Love In Fantasy

ELLE CHRISTENSEN

Created with Vellum

FOR ANYONE WHO LOVES A HAPPILY EVER AFTER.
HOW ABOUT TWELVE?

FANTASY MIRRORS DESIRE.
IMAGINATION RESHAPES IT.
—MASON COOLEY

OLIVER

I was never one to put much stock in fairy tales, love at first sight, or happy endings. They didn't seem relevant enough in my life to give a second thought. I was focused on my career, building my empire, and I had no desire to find love. In fact, I rarely even dated. I was no Prince Charming and the idea that I would find a princess was practically ludicrous. Never mind the fact that I grew up in a country still ruled by royalty; I'd left it behind long ago.

Life is full of unexpected twists and turns, but the reality is, our future is of our making, or so I thought. When Preston St. Claire, King of Rêves and my best friend's older brother, reached out to me, asking me to consider returning to my homeland, I made the decision as a professional. The country was dwindling, and without an infusion of business and tourism, it would soon sink into complete poverty. To my surprise, I realized a part of me had longed to return home.

These events were based on my decisions, my vision for the future. Turns out, that little diaper-wearing, flying bastard Cupid, was determined to prove me wrong. After several work-consumed months, I finally poked my head outside the hole I'd been in and accepted a dinner invitation at the palace. If you're picturing a gigantic medieval structure complete with turrets and a moat, keep right on imagining it. It's like something out of a movie, and speaking of movie moments, here is another one for you. I walked into the picturesque, stately home and was literally knocked on my ass by the most beautiful woman I'd ever seen.

Philippa St. Claire came barreling around a corner, and the next thing I knew, we were sprawled on the ground, and I became very aware of the lush curves pressed against my body. The smell of jasmine invaded my senses, sending a tingling straight to my groin. After helping her to her feet, I swept my gaze from top to bottom, and the tingling became a burn. She had a knockout figure with large breasts, a small waist, and flared hips, all encased in a pair of tight jeans, and a black, long-sleeved top that clung to her upper body. She was on the shorter side, maybe five foot four, making her seem even more delicate next to my six foot three frame. And yet, I had a hunch her curvy body would fit perfectly into mine. Her dark, chocolate brown hair hung from a ponytail in ringlets to the center of her back, and her sable eyes sparkled as she smiled at me. I drank in the sight of her honey-colored skin—heart-shaped face, with high cheekbones, and bee-stung lips. She was fucking gorgeous.

I wanted her. And not for a quick fuck or even one night. I wanted to be her forever. She was eighteen—the youngest of twelve sisters, including three sets of twins—so there was an eleven-year age gap between us. I didn't give a flying fuck about it; Philippa St. Claire belonged to me.

After one evening in her company, I was even more enchanted. Not only was she beautiful on the outside, but her sisters and parents clearly adored her. When she displayed some sass and wit, it only confirmed what I'd felt, and I started to formulate a plan. I made time over the next several months to visit the family often and, in particular, get Pippa and me alone so we could get to know each other. She was earning her degree in English Literature, while attempting to establish herself as an "Indie" author. Whatever that meant. She wanted to travel the world, and I was more than happy to make her dreams come true, if only she would let me.

I was relieved when I didn't notice a man spending time with her. If they came around, she sent them scurrying away with their head hanging in defeat and disappointment. It made things simpler for me since I didn't have to pull them aside and threaten them to stay away from my woman.

As time went by, her face began to light up when she first saw me. She smiled incessantly, even when we had a spat. Admittedly, they were usually my fault since I enjoyed getting her riled. She looked so fuckable when she was fired up about something.

To my frustration, however, she avoided talking about us, or relationships in general, other than the occasional smartass remark about being "tied down." I knew she'd fallen for me the instant we'd met, just as I had for her, but I had thought it best to allow her time for our relationship to build and for her to recognize her feelings on her own. Until it became clear my siren wasn't going slow at all, she was putting up a fucking roadblock.

She's mine.

OLIVER

I've finally run out of patience. I'm in a constant state of arousal every time I'm around Pippa—my cock hard and my body craving her touch. It's time to claim her. Out of respect, I took her father aside yesterday and told him of my intentions with his daughter, although, his disapproval would not have stopped me. He laughed and shook his head with mock disappointment. "Another one bites the dust." I gave him a questioning lift of my eyebrow. Instead of an explanation he said, "I wish you luck. If anyone can convince that girl to settle down, I'd put my money on you. But, I'll enjoy watching her lead you on a merry chase." He clapped me on the back and strolled from the room, still laughing. I was a little confused but didn't dwell on it.

I showed up today with flowers and an invitation to dinner. I was rendered speechless, a moment ago, when I was turned down with a bright smile and a polite "No, thank you."

It is taking a lot of effort not to let my jaw hang open in surprise. It seems my little spitfire is misunderstanding what is happening right now. I decide to try a physical explanation before a verbal one. Taking her hand, I tug her into my arms and crash my mouth down onto hers. She freezes, taken by surprise, and a little gasp gives me the opening I need. My tongue sweeps inside, and I angle my head to deepen the kiss. After a moment, she melts into the kiss and begins to respond, albeit hesitantly. A shot of even stronger arousal sparks inside me when it becomes obvious how innocent she is. It makes me want to beat my chest and yell like a caveman at the thought of being the one to teach her about pleasure.

Before I lose my control, I lift my head, smirking when I see the dazed expression on her face, and the blatant arousal in her eyes. There aren't any signs that she isn't attracted to me or doesn't feel the pull between us. If there was, I *might* have walked away. But, it clearly isn't the case, and I'm determined to get Pippa to admit to it, eventually. Sooner, rather than later.

I keep ahold of her hand and lead her over to the couch where I sit close beside her. "Pippa, let me be clear. You are mine. You have been since the moment you knocked me on my ass." I see the barest hint of a smile, despite her attempts to remain aloof.

"We've never even been on a date, Oliver. How could I possibly be yours?" she asks tartly. She scoots away, so I follow, staying in her space. Her cheeks turn bright with a pink blush, and she squirms uncomfortably. I know she is affected by me, but her glower is cluing me in that some of the color is from anger. She is sexy as hell and yet somehow manages to also be adorable. I mentally shake my head at myself. In a matter of twenty-four hours, it seems I've turned into a sap.

"You simply are, baby." I shrug, moving on since it isn't up for discussion. "You can't deny our chemistry, Pippa. You're going to be my wife and then I'm going to fuck my kid into you the minute we say I do."

Her eyes widen at my blunt words and I kiss her before she

can respond. "Then, we get our happily ever after," I whisper against her velvet-soft lips.

She pulls back and the scowl is still on her face, making me sigh. "I have no intention of becoming shackled to another person," she says with irritation. "Let alone ending up a cliché. I can't even cook, so the idea of me being barefoot and pregnant in the kitchen is utterly ridiculous. Why don't you pursue someone who will fall to her knees and beg for what you're offering?"

I grin. "Baby, have no doubt. You'll be on your knees, begging for what I've got. It's only a matter of time."

The old ball and chain

I fight the need to squirm at Oliver's statement. Maybe he isn't as stuffy as I first thought. But that doesn't mean I'm going to let him sweep me off my feet with this tall, dark, and sexy thing he has going on. His wavy black hair and ocean-blue eyes have no effect on me. I don't want to know what it would be like to have his muscular body wrapped around me, and I've already forgotten the feel of those full lips kissing mine. *I certainly didn't fall for him the moment I met him.* I mentally sigh; I don't believe me, either.

I've been fighting off admirers, or if you want to go the old-fashioned way—suitors—since I turned eighteen. It's a source of great amusement to me when they approach my father for my "hand in marriage" and he tells them to ask me. Then, I choose a colorful way in which to turn each one down. I can be quite creative, so it's always entertaining. *For me.* I have an ace in my pocket, though, and it looks like now is the time to play it.

"I can't marry you, Oliver." I tug my hand, trying to get him to let go, but his grip tightens and a low sound rumbles in his chest. Did he just growl at me? Why the hell do I find that so damn sexy? *Focus, Pippa!* "I need to get something from the desk and seeing as my hand is attached to my arm . . . do you see where I'm going with this?"

"You're gorgeous when you get feisty," he says with a grin and me melt and butterflies to flit around in my stomach. Irritated at my reaction, I pull hard and manage to get free, though I suspect it's only because he allowed it. I hurry to the little writing desk across the room and snatch a piece of paper from the top drawer. I return to my seat, leaving a cushion of space between us and shove the paper into his hands as he starts to crowd me again. He stops moving and looks down at the document he's holding. As he reads through it, his expression darkens bit by bit, and I get a little nervous about his reaction. Finally, his head lifts and his blue eyes are filled with fire, practically burning a hole through me.

"This can't possibly be valid. This law has to have been abolished; it's absolutely archaic."

I shake my head. "Nope. So you see, I have no choice but to turn you down," I say with insincere sorrow. *Mostly.* "None of the king's daughters can marry until their older sisters are married."

The incredulity on his face is almost comical until a calculating gleam enters his eyes, making me nervous again. The paper crumples in his fist as he stands. "All right, Pippa. Have it your way." He spins and stalks purposefully towards the door, leaving me feeling oddly bereft. I got what I wanted, so why am I not elated? At the door, he stops and turns back. "Is engaged acceptable?"

I shrug, holding in a laugh, realizing I was wrong. Apparently, my challenge has been accepted. The butterflies take flight once again—the little buggers. "I suppose. It doesn't really matter, Oliver. By the time all of my sisters are engaged or married, you'll have moved on."

He narrows his eyes and his gaze bores into me once again.

"I want your agreement right now," he demands. "When all of your sisters are married or engaged, you'll marry me. Willingly. Without argument."

I contemplate his likelihood for success and decide it's a safe promise to make. He'll be old and gray before all of my sisters are married. Especially Willow, who is the oldest. She is a chemist and spends all of her time in the lab. She's beautiful but doesn't care about her appearance, living in jeans, old T-shirts, and a white lab coat. I doubt anyone could open her eyes and make her take a look at the men who drool over her.

"Okay."

He smirks. "I'm going to have you, Pippa. One way or another. But, we'll play it your way for now. Just know, the reason I'm so successful is because when I want something, I go after it aggressively, and I always get it." He winks at me —*stupid butterflies*—and leaves. I'm left contemplating whether or not I want him to win.

Its name is Wilhelm

OLIVER

"Simon!" I bellow as I shove away from my desk. It's been three days since Pippa laid down the gauntlet and I'm getting ready to say fuck it, and kidnap her sexy, little ass. I approached her father first, asking him to get rid of the stupid law. He roared with laughter and puffed up with pride at his daughter's resourcefulness and imagination. I scowled, and it only made him laugh harder.

"You're going to have to beat her at her own game, Oliver. I'm too entertained to step in." His expression sobered slightly, enough to let me know his next words were not to be taken lightly. *"Or perhaps, I want to see if you are worthy of my baby girl."*

My assistant, Simon, comes running into the room looking harried and a little pissed off. I've kept him busy the last few days trying to find me a solution to this absurd situation. We couldn't find any legislation that would negate the law. As far as I knew, only one of of her sisters had a boyfriend, and from Pippa's comments, it was on the rocks. None of the others appeared to be in a relationship, much less engaged, Pippa was staunchly refusing to give in. I'd think her stubbornness was adorable if it weren't directed at me.

Tugging on my hair, I glare at the younger man, but the action is a waste as he glares right back. "Stop yelling like a fucking lunatic, Oliver. Your staff is starting to think you've lost your damn mind. Abbi has called in sick five times in the last two weeks." Abbi is my secretary, and one of Pippa's sisters, so it's probably not a good idea for me to freak her out. "Then again," he continues with an irritated glance back at my door, "even when she's here, she's exhausted and sluggish."

I feel a little guilty because I hadn't noticed this about Abbi. Maybe I have lost my mind; I'm not usually so callus. I feel like every moment without Pippa is a moment wasted, and if I don't get my ring on her finger and her body beneath mine soon, I'll lose my last thread of sanity. I'll break every law in this country, and every other country, to make her mine.

Perhaps it would be best to deal with this somewhere else. "Let's discuss this away from the office," I mutter, donning my suit jacket and heading for the door. My office building happens to be a three-minute drive from the house I'd bought after meeting Pippa. *House* is a bit of an understatement; it's more like a small castle, but the minute I saw it, I knew it belonged to Pippa. Her reaction the first time I took her there had only confirmed my instincts, and I'd enjoyed watching her explore, delighted at all the little things she discovered.

I hop in my car and start it while Simon gets into the passenger seat, then make the short drive to my home. We head inside and I hang up my coat before leading him to my office where I drop some files I brought onto my desk. I walk around it, and raise an eyebrow at Simon. "Have you found anything?" I growl, earning me another glower.

"No one wants you to get Philippa St. Claire more than I do, Oliver. Maybe then you'll work off your frustrations in other ways, rather than terrifying your staff." I'm sure I'll feel bad about this after my sanity returns. But, at the moment, I'm not in the frame of mind to care.

"Short of casting a love spell on her sisters, I'm out of ideas," I grumble as I drop down into my chair, shuffling the papers around on the desktop mindlessly. Simon is oddly silent, and after a minute, I look up curiously. He's studying me, a thoughtful, albeit wary, look on his face, his fingers pinching and twisting his lips. I raise an eyebrow. "Do you have a hidden love potion lying around, Simon?" I drawl sarcastically.

He stops abusing his lips and presses them into a thin line, shaking his head. "Not exactly."

"What do you mean 'not exactly'? Seriously, Simon? Please tell me you aren't about to suggest we go out and find ourselves a gypsy." My voice drips with sarcasm.

"Oliver," he says hesitantly, "we are out of resources. So, open your mind a little and don't discount it until I'm done explaining." He stares at me archly. "Unless you're ready to give up on having Pippa," he adds.

The thought of a life without my sassy, little temptress leaves me cold and the desperation from a few minutes ago comes rushing back. It might be far-fetched and ridiculous, but as I said before, I'll do anything to have her. I gesture for him to continue and prepare myself to keep from laughing at what I'm sure will be an entertaining suggestion. He sits in the chair on the opposite side of my desk, sprawling his legs out and getting comfortable. I roll my eyes and grunt, "Get on with it, asshole."

He scowls at my attitude, and I shrug. *Whatever.*

"When I was sifting through all of the old papers in the palace library," he begins, "I came across a page that looked as though it might have been from a journal of some sort. It referenced a key—a skeleton key—one that supposedly 'unlocks' love."

I start to scoff, but swallow it down at the annoyed frown he shoots my way. "Anyway," he snaps. "There wasn't much information, and I don't know how it works, but, in desperation to turn you back into a human being instead of this fire-breathing dragon you've become, I looked into it." His eyes shoot daggers at me, daring me to comment and I dutifully stifle my remark. "I couldn't find any more information but, there was a box in their attic, of all places, with the design of a key carved in the wood. Um..." He clears his throat and shifts in his seat uncomfortably. "I could have sworn it wasn't in the box of old documents the last several times I dug through it." He shrugs. "I went back to get it this morning, but it was gone. I couldn't open it anyway, but maybe you'd have better luck."

Finally, it appears he is finished, and I'm allowed to speak. "If it's not there anymore, why are we even having this discussion?" I query with a mock scowl.

"I thought, um," he mutters and shifts again, seemingly struggling to find his words. "Um, I thought maybe it was a, you know, *Sword in the Stone* kind of situation. If you go looking, it might show up again, and you'll be able to open it."

That does it. I roar with laughter, holding my stomach and gasping for air, tears leaking from my eyes. "*Sword in the Stone?*"

Simon leans back in his chair and watches me with an air of mild irritation. "It's worth a shot, man. What other avenues do we have?"

The thought sobers me somewhat, though I still can't wrap my head around the idea of a magical key that will help me convince Pippa to admit she loves me. I rub a finger lightly against one of my temples, trying to relieve the constant ache I've felt since I learned about the fucking edict. *Is it worth a shot?* I do a mental face plant onto my desk, the rational side of me wanting to kick my ass for even considering it. However, there is a louder voice, the one from my heart and . . . other parts of my body. This is the voice that claimed Pippa and is desperate to make her mine. Voice number two wins out. What could it hurt to take a leap of faith?

"Where was it?" I ask suspiciously.

Simon perks up, clearly happy I've decided to give this a shot. "Just in case, with the king's permission, I had the box brought over from the palace." He points to a set of wooden double doors on the wall to my left. I rarely use the closet, so I often forget the gleaming, dark, cherry wood doors are there for more than aesthetics. They match the rest of the furniture in the room, setting off the lighter, beige walls, and cream accents in the curtains and seat cushions. It's definitely a male space and I vaguely wonder if I should set up an office for Pippa or let her redecorate this one and share. The idea of being separated from her for a significant length of time, even by the walls of our home, is abhorrent to me.

The sound of three sharp claps brings me back from my musings. Simon raises his brows, his expression a little daring. Did he think I would back out? I snort. He knows me better than that. I jerk my chin towards the door. "Out," I deadpan. His incredulous face almost breaks my façade as I fight not to laugh. It feels good to find some amusement after so many days of aggravation and ire. He stands slowly, exaggerating the movement, obviously hoping I'll change my mind. Unfortunately for him, I have to do this alone. I have no desire to have an audience, even Simon, who had this ludicrous idea, when I'm confronted with my gullibility because the key is useless—if it's even there at all.

The door shuts with a click, and I open the closet to find the cardboard box sitting on the floor. Squatting down, I heft the box into my arms and take it over to my desk. I stare down at it and sigh, already regretting my decision. Then a picture of Pippa floats into my vision, and I wrench the top of the box off. I dig through the mess of papers until I find a small, oblong, wooden box, about two by six inches, with the carving of a key on the top. It's an unusual design, a skeleton key of some kind.

Taking it with me, I round my desk and sit in my chair, then place it on the desktop and stare at it. Here goes nothing. There is a small metal catch on the front, and I'm surprised when it lifts with ease. However, the top stays tightly sealed when I try to open it. *Sword in the Stone my ass.* Leaning back in my chair, I continue watching it as I brood until I realize I'm squinting through the darkness. The sun has set and I didn't notice, so all of the lights are still off.

My chair squeaks as I roll it away and stand up, gathering some papers to read over in bed. *My fucking cold and lonely bed.* I open the door and step into the hall, but before I can continue, I stop and think. Overthink and analyze, until I tell myself to shut the fuck up before I get a headache. Pivoting, I stalk back into the room and grab the small box, taking it with me to my bedroom. I set it on the dresser and go about getting ready, my eyes involuntarily drawn to it over and over. Finally, I move to stand in front of it and glare at the stupid thing. *This is ridiculous.* I roll my eyes and turn to get into bed, but freeze suddenly when the room is dimly lit by a golden light. Whipping around, I'm taken aback by the sight of the box and brightness that seems as though it's trying to escape through the cracks. I fight the need to glance at the clock on my nightstand, because if it's midnight, that would mean I've lost my mind. There would be no other explanation than I've succumbed to some sort of fairytale insanity.

I lose the fight and peer at the clock from the corner of my eye. It's official, Monsieur D'Arque should be here any time now to haul me off to the asylum for loons. The box vibrates, drawing my full attention to it once again. When I just stand here, it trembles again, a little more erratically. It calms and I take a step back, only to see it repeat the shaking, with even more force. I move closer and unlike before, when I stop, the pulsating is very faint. *What the fuck?* It's like the box was getting annoyed that I wasn't opening it. At this thought, the box practically jumps from the heavy vibration. "Ok, ok," I grumble. *Great, talking to a box.* I shake my head at this whole foolish business and reach out to lift the lid. This time, it whooshes open smoothly, standing up straight to reveal the source of the golden light. It's a key, one that matches the carving on the top of the box. I figure I might as well go all in and release my hold on any rational thought. The light dies down when I pick up the key. It's warm against my skin, but it's a little odd. If I didn't know better, I would almost describe it as body heat. *Ludicrous.*

I continue to inspect it and it looks to be made of solid gold, and weighs at least a pound. On the head, there is an intricate design—vines that create a heart. *Really?* Seems a bit on the nose, if you ask me...

What now? I'm standing here like an idiot, waiting for who the hell knows what, and talking to an inanimate object. *Fantastic.* A sudden bolt of electricity shoots through my arm and I stare disbelievingly at the key. "Did you just shock me?" The key glows a little and I double blink in shock, before sighing heavily in exasperation. *Great, a smartass, magical key.* The sound of crinkling paper breaks my stare down with the cocky little object. I look up and see a note attached to the inside of the lid, fluttering as though it were in a breeze. Taking the note, I read the words and though a part of me still wants to attribute this whole episode to being a figment of my imagination, the other part is smiling in triumph.

I begrudgingly admit that Simon was right; the purpose of the key is to help one find their love. For a brief moment, I worry it won't be of any help because I've already found her. But, as I read the instructions, it dawns on me that this is actually a solution for the predicament my little temptress has stuck me in. The key will unlock the fantasies of each sister, and they'll discover who their true love is. It's corny, I know, but it's not like I wrote it, so stop judging.

I can only imagine her reaction when she realizes I've plowed through her eleven barriers. Knowing my Pippa, it ought to be entertaining, and mutually satisfying when it ends with her screaming as she falls apart in my arms.

"All right, Wilhelm," I address the key, christening it with the name of one of the Brothers Grimm (it seemed appropriate). "We'll start tomorrow night with Willow." I groan. I need to stop talking to the key; it can't be good for my level of sanity.

A motherfucking fairy godmother

OLIVER

My eyes blink open as sunlight fills my bedroom. I laugh to myself over the ridiculous dream I had. *If only*, I think. Wouldn't it be nice to have a magical way to fix this predicament? After dreaming about the key, I had a vivid dream about Pippa's oldest sister and the guy she dated in high school, James Pierce. He was the same year as me (one year ahead of Willow). We were friends, though not close ones. When he graduated, his parents decided to sell the farm he grew up on and travel the world, but they'd died in a car crash a few months later.

Since James had a scholarship in the United States, in a prestigious pre-med program, it made sense for him to take it. She went to Oxford to become a chemical engineer. We all thought they—of all people—would make long distance work. But he never returned from the states and it seems she's been single ever since.

As it happens, she currently works for my company. She must have been on my mind and that was the reason I dreamt about her and James.

Flinging the covers off of my body, I hop up and walk to

my dresser to grab clothes on my way to the shower. Lost in thought, I open drawers and take the things I need, then come to a sudden stop. I blink a few times, but every time my eyes adjust, I see the same thing. The small, wooden box is sitting open on the top of the bureau, the odd key nestled in black velvet. It must have sprung open in the night. The moment I turn away, I hear a familiar humming, the sound of vibrations. My head twists and I stare at the key, beginning to accept that, apparently, it wasn't a dream. What to do with this knowledge, I'm not sure. I wander to the bathroom and take a hot shower, fully waking myself. Once I'm ready for work, I make my way to the kitchen where my housekeeper has left me a steaming pot of coffee. Reading the morning paper, I drink the hot liquid and try not to think about the thing . . . in the box . . . in my room.

I finish and put my cup in the sink before retrieving my briefcase from my office, ready to leave for work. At the door to the garage, I once again find myself pausing. I've done nothing but run through scenarios this morning, no matter how much I tried not to, and I keep coming up with the same conclusion: what have I got to lose? As long as I keep this whole magic and fantasy stuff to myself, of course. I jog back up to my room and take the key from the case, receiving a little zap as I pick it up. Something tells me it's protesting almost being left behind. *Oh, right. Wilhelm has an attitude.* I drop the key into the breast pocket of my suit coat, then dash back downstairs and out to my car. I arrive just in time for a meeting, which leads to another and another, until the day is almost done. As my employees clock out, I take the opportunity to work uninterrupted for a while.

A knock on my door startles me and I look up to see . . . James? Wilhelm hums in my pocket. *Interesting.* "James," I greet. "Come on in." I gesture for him to take a seat.

"Thanks. I apologize for interrupting." He settles his

frame in a leather, high-backed chair, facing me and stretches his long legs out in front of him. He is about my height, but I notice he seems much leaner, almost as though he is smaller boned than he used to be. He runs his hands through his dark-blond hair, another change, his hair was several shades lighter when we were teenagers.

"It's been a while," I remark, leaning back into my plush leather chair. "What can I do for you?"

"Yes, it has." James frowns as he leans forward to rest his elbows on his knees, then steeples his fingers. "But, it was time I came home. I probably should have applied and sent you a resume, like all of the other stiffs applying for a job, but here I am anyway." His mouth quirks up in a crooked smile that doesn't reach his brown eyes before opening a folder I didn't realize he was carrying, then slides a sheet of paper across the desk.

I pick it up and scan it. His resume is certainly impressive. However, on my second glance, I stop at a gap of time where he has no listed employment. I look closely and realize I missed it the first time because it isn't blank. The time is filled with what looks like an internship working with a trial program in... "Cancer research?" I ask curiously. I'd thought his specialty was anesthesiology.

James nods, his steady gaze never leaving mine. I don't know what it is about his look, his countenance, but a thought enters my mind and won't go away. "Were you a participant?" I ask.

"Yes. It was an experimental treatment for cancer patients who were given a terminal diagnosis."

"Well, fuck, James," I breathe, "I had no idea."

He shakes his head, a rueful frown on his face. "Nobody did. You know I don't have any family left, and I preferred not to have my friends and . . . other people, watching me waste away as their last memory of me."

My head cocks to the side and I study him thoughtfully. I can see his point, but he'd taken the choice away from everyone. People who probably would have preferred to be by his side until the end. And, knowing exactly who this "other people" is, I wouldn't want to be him when he has this conversation with her.

"Well, I'm glad you made it," I tell him honestly. "You know you've got a job here, if you want it. Go and talk to the head of HR and we'll find something that fits both our needs."

"Thanks," he says, then his face clouds with some dark emotion. "I don't want to disrupt her life, so I'll stay out of her way," he informs me. "I'm sure she moved on a long time ago."

I don't respond, particularly because the last comment seemed to be introspective. We both stand and shake hands. "Let's catch up some time," he suggests, his voice genuine, and his smile reaching his eyes for the first time since he stepped into my office.

"Absolutely," I agree, returning his smile. "The next twelve days will be . . . busy, but catch me after and we'll go for a beer."

With a nod and a wave, he departs from my office and I sit down to get back to work. Fifteen minutes later, a throat clears and I look up to see Willow standing in the doorway. All of the St. Claire girls favor each other, though they have varying shades of dark hair and green eyes. However, Willow looks the least like Pippa, her dark hair short and straight, and her eyes a brighter green. Yet, if they were together, no one would have any doubt they were sisters. I wave her in and she removes her suit jacket before sitting in the chair James recently vacated.

"I heard James Pierce is back," she states without preamble.

"Yes," I confirm, curious what her reaction will be.

"I'd um—I'd rather not work with him. If you don't mind," she says hesitantly. "I don't want anything to do with him. He obviously hasn't felt anything for me in a long time."

"Done." I nod to accentuate my agreement. They will be in completely different departments of the company anyway. The last thing I need right now is drama from star-crossed lovers. Besides, it looks as though I'll be helping her find her true love soon. *I sound like a motherfucking fairy godmother.*

"Thanks," she murmurs as she gets to her feet. "By the way," she adds with a smirk. "My sisters and I are rooting for you. We think you're good for Pippa and we've done our best to sway her." Her smile turns rueful. "But she's stubborn as an ox. Good luck, Oliver." With a small wave, she leaves, turning in the direction of her office.

I lean back in my chair, contemplating the circumstances of the day. My wandering eyes land on the empty chair and I realize she's left her jacket hanging on the back. She appeared to be going back to her office, so I think I can catch her. I'm ready to head out for the day and grab my things. As I pick up her coat, I suddenly imagine myself dropping Wilhelm into her pocket. The thought sets the little bugger humming and I take it out and slip it into her jacket.

Wait . . . *Did that little fucker just Jedi mind trick me?* I groan silently to myself. *This is really getting out of hand.*

Tossing the piece of clothing over my arm, I set off for the back of the building where there are offices and labs. When I find her alone, I frown. "You left your coat." I hold it up for emphasis. She smiles in thanks as I hang it on the hook beside the door. "Make sure somebody walks you to your car tonight, Willow. Royalty or not, it's all the same to someone bent on doing harm."

"I'll have a security guard escort me," she agrees. I stare her down for a moment, trying to decide if she's taking me seriously. When I'm satisfied that she is, I lift my chin in farewell and head out to my car. Once I'm inside and driving home, a question occurs to me—how will I get Wilhelm back? *Shit.*

I get home and find myself spending the evening brooding in my library, sipping on scotch and staring at my fireplace. My vision is getting fuzzy, and I blink a few times to clear it, because what I think I'm seeing can't possibly be what I'm really seeing. Images in the flames? For fuck's sake, is this *Harry Potter* now? I had hoped we'd confined this lunacy to fairy tales.

A glance at the clock above the mantle tells me it's a few minutes after midnight. It's not exactly shocking, at this point. I look back to the fire and the images—no—the movie has become clear, almost as though it's being projected onto the flames. That's when I realize, it's my fantasy. Okay. This is more like it. I refill my drink and relax into my comfy chair, visions of my woman and our life together dancing in my head.

Meanwhile...

Willow's Fantasy

AS YOU WISH

Willow lifts her head from where it was cradled in her arms on her desk and looks around, confused at finding herself still in her office at work. She sighs, so desperate to avoid her empty, lonely home, she fell asleep at her desk, again. She can't avoid it forever, so she stands and lifts her purse over her shoulder, then meanders over to her jacket, hanging by the closed door. Lifting it off the hook, she notices a distinct weight on one side and realizes there is something in the pocket. She reaches inside and her fingers wrap around a cool object that causes a tingle in her hand as she pulls it out. It's a key. A very unusual key.

She doesn't know where it's come from, but for some reason, it feels at home in her palm. *Odd.* She decides to worry about it in the morning, putting the key back in the pocket and draping the coat over her arm. She opens the door to her office and pauses in shock. Rather than the neutral-toned walls and grey carpet of her office hallway, she finds herself standing in a foyer. It's tall and round, the walls covered in an intricate, gold-swirled pattern, with a cream, travertine floor, and ornate sconces that match the ambiance. Not to mention the sparkling chandelier hanging in the center.

She looks around in awe, her jaw practically on the ground, until her gaze locks onto a set of carved, gold double doors. Without thinking, she steps towards them, giving into a pull she feels, knowing there is something special beyond them. The key glows brighter the closer she comes to the doors and she spies a lock with a small engraving above it. It matches the key. Despite a small, rational part of her brain warning her to be wary, curiosity and an overwhelming sense of rightness have her unlocking the door and swinging it open.

Leaving the key in the lock, she steps into the family room of an unknown castle and gasps. It's beautiful, but comfortable and lived in. Somehow, she knows this place is everything she could have imagined for her dream home. It even has scattered toys all around to indicate a child or children live here. Her every wish, deepest desires, and perfect fantasy have always been to have a home and family. She didn't need a prince; she wanted her own sweet farm boy. She'd always assumed she would live in her family home when she became queen, but this, this is really what her heart desires—a place that belongs to her and her little family.

Walking into it with trepidation, she jumps when the door behind her closes and glances back to see it's disappeared. Her heart speeds up with nervousness and she calls out, "Hello?" She immediately hears the sound of footsteps coming towards the room. The doorway is suddenly filled by the overwhelming presence of the man she's loved since she was fifteen years old.

"Hey, buttercup," he says with a gentle smile, walking towards her, his eyes twinkling with . . . love? Buttercup? He used to call her that all the time, telling her she looked like the blooms in spring rather than a drooping tree. He reaches her and pulls her into his arms, planting a scorching kiss on her still mute mouth. She is helpless to keep from melting into him, remembering what this used to feel like, and realizing she's been craving it ever since she lost it. It's followed by a rush of love so intense, it consumes her. Apparently, she hadn't moved on as far as she thought she had if it was so easy for him to bring it all crashing back.

James finally lets her up for air and his mouth tips up into a crooked smile. "You slept a long time, buttercup"—he winks roguishly—"I hope you were dreaming of me." *Had she been napping?* His beautiful mouth grows into a grin and he pats her stomach. "Is my boy wearing you out?" Willow's head snaps down to stare at her belly and, sure enough, there is a little baby bump. *What the fuck?* She looks back up at James and he eyes her curiously. "You're not going to argue with me about it being a girl?" he asks in mild surprise.

"Um..." She scrambles for what to say, then remembers. They used to argue about the kids they would have. He joked that he was made to breed superheroes and predicted they would only have boys. She told him to get over himself and buy a shotgun because being scared to raise daughters didn't mean she was going to pop out the cast of *The Avengers*. Besides, it was enough that their children would be princes and princesses, they didn't need to add superpowers to the mix.

"I don't want to argue," she blurts.

He raises a brow questioningly, but then shrugs with a smile. "As you wish."

A picture on the wall behind him, of two familiar little boys, draws her attention and before she knows it, it all comes screaming back to her. James showing up after he graduated from college, proposing, their wedding, and the birth of their two rowdy little boys. Had she been dreaming of his leaving with a promise to return and then never coming back? Was all of the time apart—the pain and heartache—all a nightmare? "I had the most vivid nightmare," she tells him in a trembling voice, tears gathering in her eyes.

"Hey now, Willow," he soothes as he runs a hand over her hair and kisses her forehead. "Don't cry. Want to tell me about it?"

She begins to cry in earnest and he scoops her up, taking her to the couch and holding her while she sobs into his shirt. "You—you left and didn't come back. No explanation, nothing. When I tried to contact you, you were just . . . gone. Never to be heard from again." Her tears begin to thin and she stares up at him, her eyes containing all of the despair from years of a broken heart. "For eleven years," she sniffles. "You must have gone through your cancer all alone. In fact, in my dream, I never even knew about it. I—I don't want to rule without you."

"Shhh, it was just a dream, buttercup," he says, placing soft kisses all over her face. "I'm here. What did I tell you when I left?" He grasps her chin so she is forced to look him in the eye.

"Listen to me, what we have is true love. I will always come for you," she repeats his words from when he left.

"You were what kept me going. Always. You're mine, Willow. I'll never let you go." His mouth crashes down on hers and she feels his love surrounding her. She revels in it, letting it wrap her up like a heated blanket, warming her from the years of cold and loneliness.

"Ewwww!" The disgusted voice of a child breaks them apart and Willow flushes with embarrassment. Their little four-year-old boy, Eric, stands with his feet apart and his little fists planted on his hips. "Do you guys hab to do dat? It's gwoss."

Willow starts giggling as James snickers in her ear, "Cutest little cock blocker in the world," he whispers. Then to Eric he says, "Yup, I have to kiss your mommy. Don't you want another brother?" He grunts when Willow jabs her elbow into his stomach.

Eric's eyes squint as he thinks hard about the question. "You hab to kiss mommy for me to get anodder brodder?" James nods solemnly. Eric shrugs. "Okay." He spins around to leave but calls out, "Be careful, Daddy. My friend Jason says girls hab cooties. Even Pwincess Buwwercwup."

James laughs then nibbles on Willow's ear, causing a shiver to run down her spine and her panties to become damp. Her breath catches when his hand slides up her skirt, beneath her underwear, and one long finger dips inside her pussy. "You have the best cooties, buttercup." She whimpers as he extracts his hand, bringing it to his mouth and sucking it clean. He licks his lips and his eyes scorch her with promises she knows she'll have to wait for him to fulfill. "Tonight, when the boys are gone for their sleepover at your sister's house, I'm going to remind you that you're mine. I'll fuck the nightmares right out of your head."

He stands with Willow still cradled in his arms, then lets her feet swing down so that her body lowers along his inch by inch. Embers of desire have been glowing and now they have ignited into a steady flame, heating her from the inside out. "I missed you," she whispers.

James looks confused for a moment, then a look of understanding crosses his face and he hugs her tightly. "If in some fucked up universe, I really let you go, then I missed you more, because I was the monumentally stupid ass who gave up the one thing in life he valued more than anything else. But, I have no doubt, eventually, I would have come for you. Like I promised."

Willow smiles and kisses his lips softly, then jumps away when the loud ring of the doorbell slices through the quiet.

"I'll get it! I'll get it! I'll get it!" Eric squeals as he races towards the front door.

"Eric, we don't open the door without asking who is there," she chides and he drops his hands from the doorknob with a sheepish grin.

"It's not like he didn't know it was me," a voice calls through the door. Willow rolls her eyes and marches to the door, flinging it open. Her sister Chloe, the next one down in the lineup, stands on the porch grinning. A large, muscular man stands protectively behind her. With his light brown skin, dark eyes, and long, inky-black hair in a braid down his back, he resembles the societal ideal of an American Indian. Damon is Cherokee, in fact, and next to her pale skin, dark, reddish-brown hair, and sea-green eyes, they make a striking couple.

Although, they aren't really a *couple*, in the romantic sense of the word. Chloe is a singer and had recently been having problems with "overly-friendly" fans. She hired Damon to protect her. His eyes never stray far from Chloe, but it's obvious he is completely aware of his surroundings. It's also glaringly obvious that Chloe is ignoring him. It's *inconceivable* that these two don't recognize the sparks flying between them. Unless they are choosing to ignore them. *Which is stupid.*

"I'm trying to teach him good habits, Chlo. You think you could go along with it and stop being a trouble maker?" Willow asks with exasperation. "I'm going to need Miracle Max to brainwash the kid after you're done with him," she mutters, then she smiles over Chloe's shoulder. "Hey Damon, you got stuck on babysitting duty tonight?"

"Same as every night," he says gruffly and James coughs to cover a laugh while Chloe fumes. To Willow's amazement, though, Chloe refrains from responding to the insult.

"So, where is my other handsome man?" she asks brightly.

"He was napping, but he's probably up by now," James says.

"Would you get him?" Willow asks James over her shoulder.

"Sure, buttercup. As you wish." He kisses Willow's neck before walking away.

"You got everything, bud?" Chloe asks Eric.

"Yup!"

"Kee!!" another little high pitched voice practically screams in excitement. Chloe turns and sees her almost two-year-old nephew, Nate, struggling in his father's hold, reaching for his aunt. James barely manages to keep him from flinging himself away before he's able to hand him off to Chloe. She grins widely, "Auntie is the best job. I'll spoil you two rotten and bring you back for Mom and Dad to deal with tomorrow."

Willow rubs her temples and groans, "Chloe, I swear on *your* life, if you bring them back hopped up on candy and ice cream again, I'll be pouring sugar over your grave." She points a finger at Damon. "You're supposed to protect her, Fezzik, so keep her from turning my precious babies into little monsters or her life will be in danger," she snaps. Damon rolls his eyes, but nods. They gather up the kids and the mountain of stuff that always accompanies them, and leave for their "sweepober."

As they drive off, James waves and yells, "Have fun storming the castle!" Willow laughs and rolls her eyes at James as she waves to the kids as well. When they are no longer in sight, James shuts the door and spins Willow around, shoving her up against the door and attacking her lips. "Fuck," he pants as he rips his mouth away. "I need to be inside you, Willow." His mouth trails down her neck as he unbuckles his belt and lowers the zipper on his jeans. He takes his cock out, long and thick, it's tip already red and angry looking. Willow moans at the sight and James swallows it in a deep kiss, his hands palming her ass and lifting her off of the ground,

37

forcing her legs to circle his hips. His cock rubs along the fabric separating it from her wet heat. "Who do you belong to, Willow?" he asks raggedly.

"You," she whimpers, rubbing against him restlessly. "I've always been yours."

"And, you'll be mine forever," he grunts. "Do you want me inside you, buttercup?" he asks tightly. She nods frantically, unable to speak. "As you wish," he answers as he releases one ass cheek to shove her panties aside and thrust deep into her pussy. "Fuck, yes!" he shouts. Mindless with passion, he begins to pound into her, every one of her screams of ecstasy fueling his energy, urging him to mark her, brand her so she and everyone else will always know who owns her body and her heart.

A gossamer fog surrounds them, as though, together, they create magic and it heightens their senses. Everything is more.

"I'm—I, I'm coming!" she cries. James slips a finger between them and rubs her little bud furiously.

"Come, buttercup. Come all over my cock," he purrs.

Willow explodes into a burst of light, heat engulfing her, like she's landed on the sun. James pumps a few more times before he plants himself deep inside her and shouts her name as he fills her with his come. Their bodies are shaking and sweaty, their hearts pounding, but James kisses her gently and whispers, "I've never stopped loving you, Willow. Please forgive me."

James comes awake with a start and looks around, finding himself still in his new office. He blows out a breath of air, overwhelmed by the dream he just had and the suffocating desire for it to be real. It had taken him years, but eventually, he realized what a fucking idiot he'd been to let Willow go.

Now he was home and he was going to claim her once and for all, remind her that he'd promised to always come for her, especially after living out that little fantasy, the one where he'd returned after college to create a life with her, a home, children, all the things they had once planned for. And, fuck, he'd almost come from the dream alone. He'd fight "to the pain" for her. If he had to deal with the shriek of every child—every babe that wept in fear at his approach, every woman that cries "Dear God, what is that thing?" reverberating forever in his perfect ears, he would.

Sighing, he pushes to his feet, grabs his keys, and heads to the parking lot, dreading the solitary evening ahead of him. He gets a little turned around at some point, and finds himself in a hall with office doors lining each side from beginning to end. They are mostly dark, but one has a light on and he strolls to it. Finding it unlocked, he cautiously and quietly opens it. Time seems to stand still as he drinks in the sight before him.

Willow lies with her head on her arms, asleep on her desk. She is every bit as beautiful as she had been in his fantasies. He knows he should probably leave but his feet move of their own volition, taking him to her. He brushes her hair back from her forehead and kisses it, softly calling her name. Then, he moves down to kiss her lovely pink lips. Her eyes slowly open and she looks at him with a smile, love shining in her eyes. He'd expected anger, pain, anything but this. Sitting up, she cups his face in both hands and kisses him sweetly, chuckling when she pulls back and sees his wide-eyed shock.

"We're going to talk," she says sternly. "You've got a lot to make up for, and a lot of explaining to do. But, I know in my heart that I'll forgive you eventually, and I see no reason for both of us to suffer even more in the process." Then, her voice and expression soften. "But, I don't want to waste any more time. I want to start building the future we always fantasized about."

James sweeps her into his arms. "As you wish," he whispers before kissing her passionately, not one to question a gift so precious. It won't be easy to conquer their past, but his buttercup is his true love and, eventually, they'll get their happily ever after. It seems dreams really do come true.

One down, ten to go

OLIVER

I'm absolutely dragging this morning, having spent a good portion of my night fantasizing about Pippa. I wonder if she was dreaming about me? I'm going to pay her a visit this evening and make sure I'm all she's thinking about when she goes to bed tonight.

I'm about to leave for work when I remember Wilhelm. I don't know how to get him back and I need him to continue working through Pippa's sisters. Maybe there is something in the box that will give me a clue. I jog up the stairs to my bedroom, hurry over to the box, and open the lid. *What the fuck?*

The key is resting in his little bed of velvet. I start to wonder how, then realize I shouldn't even try to comprehend what's happening. I grab him and put him in my breast pocket again. *I'm going to go with the flow.*

That evening, as I'm getting ready to leave, James and Willow stop by my office. I'm a little surprised at their request for a leave of absence and their news that they are working things out between them. And yet, I know I shouldn't be. I mean, if I'm going to believe in a fucking magical key, I might as well believe in its abilities. Besides, now I'm one step closer to my Pippa.

Sweet dreams are made of these

PIPPA

I hit the delete button over and over and over, until the pages on the computer screen before me are blank. I'm trying to work on my novel but every time I stop to read what I've written, the characters look remarkably like Oliver and me. I may have actually called the hero Oliver a few times.

Ugh. After spending the night in the throes of erotic fantasies about him, I suppose I shouldn't be surprised. I can't even escape him in my sleep! I admit, I've often fantasized about him, but my imagination has never been so vivid, and definitely not as creative as it was last night. Despite all of the reading I do and research for the sexy scenes in my novels, there were definitely some things in my dreams I'll be adding to my erotic repertoire.

Just thinking about my dreams from the night before, my body flushes with heat. I decide to take a break and skip down the stairs from my little writing nook in the attic. Not paying attention, I plow right into a hard body—warm arms close around me, holding me steady. Hot breath bathes my ear and I shiver as a low voice says, "If you want to be slammed into by me, baby, all you have to do is agree to marry me."

I rear back, scowling and trying to break his hold, but he doesn't let me go. Before I can open my mouth and snap a caustic reply, we are interrupted by Chloe and her bodyguard, Damon, as they walk into the room, bickering, as usual. Well, Chloe's bickering; Damon only responds from time to time, otherwise wearing his usual *don't-fuck-with-me* expression and practically ignoring her. These two are the only ones who can't see the raging attraction between them. It's ridiculous.

Oliver's arms loosen and I take the opportunity to reluctantly—I mean—happily step away. I sternly lecture myself about the future I'd have with Oliver. I don't need a man controlling my every move, no matter how sexy his alpha ways are. He doesn't fight me when I scoot away. However, he does grab my hand, only allowing me to go so far. I peek at his face and see him watching Chloe and Damon thoughtfully.

The Next Contestant

OLIVER

Wilhelm is practically singing in my pocket when Chloe and Damon enter the room. I figured Chloe would be the next contestant on *Love Connection*, but by Wilhelm's little routine, seems like Damon is about to fall head over heels. I contemplate how to get the key to Chloe, then mentally shrug. I'm sure Wilhelm will let me know when the right opportunity is in front of me.

I drag Pippa out to the gardens for a walk, noticing how weak her protests are, and trying not to gloat. I take her to her favorite spot by a fountain that depicts a scene from a fairy tale about twelve sisters who dance each night away. Her father has a twisted sense of humor.

Sitting on one of the stone benches, I settle her onto my lap, swallowing any protests she has with my mouth. I then spend the next fifteen minutes reminding her who she belongs to. It takes no time at all for her to melt and become an active participant as we make out like teenagers, until I am so worked up, I know I have to leave. The first time she turned me down, I made the decision not to make love to her until we were married. I'm determined that when our bodies finally become

51

one, our hearts and souls will already be there. I'm not above using everything else to convince her, though.

She walks me to the front of the house and I give her a long, lingering kiss, completely satisfied by the dazed look on her face when I'm done. The front door suddenly swings open and Chloe comes down the steps, followed by her ever-present shadow. Wilhelm starts vibrating, and when Chloe pulls me into a hug, I take the opportunity to slip the key into her purse. "She never shuts up about you," she whispers. "You're doing just fine, don't give up." Then, she steps back and winks at me, her smile broadening when she glances at Pippa, who is standing with her arms across her chest, glaring at Chloe.

I reluctantly head home, fervently wishing I was taking my woman with me, and hoping Wilhelm knows what the fuck he's doing. Then, I spend the rest of the night dreaming about her.

Meanwhile...

Chloe's Fantasy

THE OLD BAT WAS REALLY ONTO SOMETHING.

Damon unlocks Chloe's front door and steps in first, doing a quick check, before giving her the all-clear to enter. Chloe silently follows him inside, having dutifully waited without complaint. She'd hired Damon for a reason, and it would be ridiculous not to let him do his job. Except for the times when he was truly a pain in the ass.

"It's late," she says with a sigh. "I'm going to bed." He nods and watches her go, waiting until she reaches the top step before turning and going down another hallway that leads to his room.

She likes Damon, most of the time. When they first met, she'd hoped they could be friends, and sometimes, she'd thought they were. The moments were fleeting, though, and she'd pretty much given up trying. Sometimes his tall, dark, and silent routine got on her nerves, and the sizzling attraction she felt—which was clearly not reciprocated—only made everything more complicated and hard to navigate. It tended to poke at her until she ended up irritated and, if she was honest with herself, quite bitchy. It never seemed to faze him though. She supposed she should be grateful for his vigilance; he'd kept her safe when a stalker had almost killed her.

She'd been a rising star as the lead singer of a British pop group since she was seventeen and was full steam ahead, always. But, after the first attempt on her life, she'd hired Damon. After the second, she backed off from the public scene.

Now, she is ready to retire, though early in her career, she is simply exhausted and wants to do something out of the limelight. Although, this means her need for a bodyguard is pretty much non-existent. Despite their odd relationship, she's going to miss him. Or, maybe it's simply the constant presence of someone (not necessarily him) that she'll miss. Truthfully, she has no clue where her life is going or what she really wants, but she does know she is lonely.

Walking into her bedroom, Chloe sets her purse on her dresser, then digs through it, looking for her phone. Her hand bumps something hard and cool. Running through the list of things she keeps in there, she has no idea what it could be. Lifting it out, she stares at the golden skeleton key, wondering where the hell it came from. It starts to glow a little and she almost drops it, but her mind disagrees with her bodily reflexes because her hand closes tightly around it, instead. She jumps when her bedroom door suddenly slams shut and looks around wildly for what might have caused it. Spying an open window, she wracks her brain trying to remember if she'd left it open. *Better safe than sorry.* She dashes to the door, intending to call out for Damon. Throwing her door open, she comes to a screeching halt, finding herself suddenly inside an opulent foyer with a massive set of double doors directly across from her.

Her hand tingles and she looks down, remembering the key she's holding. Curiosity overcomes her and she crosses the stone floor to the ornate doors. The lock bears a carving matching the look of her key, so she inserts it and twists. The tumblers click, indicating the door is open. She pulls the handle and steps into . . . no, it can't be. Stepping over the threshold, she rotates in a slow circle to examine, what is clearly, a bedroom meant to look as though it's in the turret of a medieval castle. Completing the three hundred and sixty-degree turn, she stands in awe for a moment. A click breaks the silence, and she spins back to the door, but it's gone. Only the rough stone of the rounded walls remains. Weird. Ok, so she's trapped. Irritated, she marches over to the large bed, covered in embroidered silk and flops down on her back with a huff, staring at the matching curtains hung on the canopy. *Well, this is a pickle.* The room doesn't have any more doors, but there are several large, arched windows in the stone walls. She approaches one to see if it can be used as a means of escape.

Yeah, that would a be a fuck no. Her fear of heights has her staggering backward, dizzy from looking down at least twenty stories. It's dark out, but the moon shines bright and illuminates the endless fall to the ground. *Was that a moat?* Returning to the bed and resuming her position from before, she breathes deep, trying to calm her racing heart. Her concentration makes her sleepy and soon she is drifting, but a clatter outside one of the windows quickly brings her fully awake.

She knows she should go find out what the noise is, but well . . . it's out the window. I'm sure you can see the predicament. Attempting to climb off of the bed, Chloe's legs get tangled in her gown. *Wait, gown?* Her eyes drop to her clothes, and she stares in shock at the long, shimmering, opaque material. Obviously a nightgown, but it reminds her of the ones Pippa describes the "blushing brides" wearing in the historical romances she reads. There is a tall mirror propped against the wall next to the bed, and she turns to examine herself. *If these were what those chicks were wearing . . . "blushing," indeed.*

There is a hazy quality to the fabric, but her figure, her nipples, and the darker area between her legs are clearly made out. The lack of underwear isn't shocking, though, since she rarely wears it anyway. If she pulls her hair forward, it will cover— Well, that's new. Her hair, which is usually a curly mess that ends just above her shoulders, is now flowing out behind her like the train of a wedding gown. Her eyes dart around once more, trying to figure out what the hell is going on and it occurs to her that reading all of Pippa's smutty historical romances must be affecting her dreams. Because this *has* to be a dream. Right?

Someone starts to climb through one of the windows, and Chloe frantically looks for something to cover herself with. She takes hold of the silk coverlet on the bed, only to realize it's a heavy quilt. She has to put all of her strength into tugging it in her direction. She isn't quick enough and the spread is only halfway off when a man drops to his feet in the room. She recognizes him immediately and forgets all about her fight with the stubborn quilt. He faces her and his dark eyes flare with heat, causing her nipples to pebble and moisture to gather between her legs. His eyes fall to her breasts and darken even further at the sight of the hardened peaks.

Chloe fidgets, feeling exposed and unbelievably turned on. She may be famous and have a great amount of confidence in many areas, but, she is still a virgin. It doesn't help her hormones to see he is only wearing breeches (which leave nothing to the imagination, by the way), and his muscular chest is bare, his ebony hair loose, hanging down his back. His beauty and masculinity are as intimidating as they are incredible. Ok . . . so the historical aspect of the fantasy makes more sense now.

"Um, what—what's going on, Damon?" she stutters.

He begins to prowl towards her, his gaze fierce, like an animal stalking its prey. When he's inches away, she loses the battle with her bravado and backs up to put more space between them. *Does he have to look so fucking delicious?*

"As long as you are free, you are in danger," he says. "I will always protect you."

Her back hits the wall and he continues to close the gap between their bodies.

"I find this puts me in a dilemma, Chloe. Because if I don't have you soon, I'll lose my ability to deem who is a threat and instead, I'll start killing every man who so much as looks at you."

"Ok," she squeaks as his big body presses into hers, his arms on either side of her head, effectively trapping her in. "I thought, ahem." She clears her throat nervously. "I thought you weren't affected by me."

His eyes glitter with hunger, the fire only growing as he stares into her sea-green pools. "I can't protect you if we are together. All I'd be able to see when I looked at you is the image of the last time I fucked you," he growls. "Keeping completely away was the only way I could shut my desire for you down and focus on my job."

"What you're telling me is that you've locked the long-haired princess in a tower in order to keep her to yourself?" she asks sassily.

His eyes dance with amusement. "I've decided to remove all other variables, Chloe." He leans his face down until his mouth is only a breath away. "I've stolen you away, you belong to me, and I'm keeping you. No one can get to you here but me, so I no longer have the duty of being your bodyguard."

"Aren't you supposed to free the princess from being hidden away by the witch?"

He grins. "I decided the old bat was really onto something." His mouth covers hers and he kisses her with such passion, she feels the flames lick her body from head to toe. He runs his tongue along the seam of her lips and she opens, accepting his tongue as it plunges inside. When he finally releases her mouth, they are both panting, their hearts galloping at full speed.

"I know you want me, Chloe," he grunts, grinding his hips into her and letting her feel what she does to him. She mewls an agreement, no longer focused on anything beyond how he's making her feel. "I will not allow anyone to take you away from me, nor will I let you escape. You will stay here and I will worship your body every chance I get, love your heart completely, and be everything and anything you will ever need."

The clouds of desire dissipate enough for her to grasp on to his statement, laser focusing on one part. "Love me?" she asks.

He nods slowly, locking his gaze with hers, letting her see his sincerity. "I love you, Chloe."

Her heart practically explodes with emotion, as though a dam broke and she realizes she's been holding them all back, afraid to let them free. Love for him pours from her heart and she slides her hands into his silky hair, taking hold with a tight grip. "I love you, too," she tells him earnestly.

His face transforms with the most beautiful smile she has ever seen. Damon has rarely ever smiled, but this, this is like a rainbow. Rare, elusive, and magical to see. After a moment, a hint of vulnerability creeps into his gaze. "You'll stay with me?"

"For as long as you love me."

He grins as he lifts her by the hips, wrapping her legs around his waist and falling with her onto the bed, his body covering hers. "So, forever then."

There are no more words. Damon whips her gown above

her head and closes his lips around one turgid nipple. Chloe moans and shifts her hips restlessly.

"Damon," she whimpers, "I need—I..."

"I know what you need, Chloe," he growls, "and I'm going to give it to you." He waves a hand and she sucks in a breath when her arms involuntarily fly up to the headboard and silk ties bind them to the posts on either side. Wow. *Magic has never seemed so sexy.* "But, I won't be rushed. I've waited so long to have you, to lick and taste every inch of this spectacular body, to sink my cock into your soaking wet pussy."

He punctuates his words with a little swivel of his hips and it's enough to set her off. She splinters apart with a cry of his name and reaches a high she didn't know existed. Floating back down, she opens her eyes to see Damon staring at her with both hunger and awe. "Watching you come is the most fucking beautiful thing I've ever seen."

Chloe blushes and it widens his smile before he kisses her again, stealing her soul with every breath. Her eyes drop to his lower body, narrowing on the breeches separating her from his, um, powerful sword? Chloe mentally giggles at herself, just keeping with the theme. It occurs to her right then, shouldn't she get magic, too?

In half a heartbeat, Damon is gloriously naked. He raises a single eye brow and a grin slowly grows on his face. Then he spends, what seems like an eternity, doing exactly what he said, worshipping, licking, and tasting her everywhere. Until finally, he sinks deep, deep inside her.

He doesn't seem surprised when he breaks through her barrier, but he does look a little smug. If Chloe weren't so fully in the throes of passion, she probably would have smacked him upside the head. As it is though, they are both lost to the feel of their bodies so completely connected.

"You're mine now, Chloe" Damon whispers once they've

come down off of the high and are cuddled in each other's arms. "Forever."

⁓

Damon shoots up into a sitting position, disoriented and confused at first, then seriously pissed when he realizes he's in bed and it was all just a fantasy. Throwing off the covers, he stands and begins to pace, sexually frustrated and his heart pounding. Maybe it's time to take the next step. The waiting is slowly killing him. Making a split second-decision, he takes off down the hall and sprints up the stairs two at a time. As he's reaching for the door handle to Chloe's room, the door flies open and she smacks right into him.

Her head comes up, meeting his gaze as his arms close around her.

"You're fired."

"I quit."

They speak over each other and it takes a minute for them to absorb what the other has said. Then Damon sweeps her into his arms, muttering, "Thank fuck," and stalks back towards her bed.

Several hours later, Damon looks down at the woman who has starred in all of his fantasies as she lies draped across his chest. With a finger under her chin, he lifts her head so their eyes meet. "You know you're going to marry me, right?" he asks gruffly.

Chloe smiles softly, leans up to kiss him, and winks. "Since you asked so nicely."

"It wasn't a request," he grumbles.

Oliver - 2, Pippa — 0

OLIVER

When I wake up this morning, the first thing I do is check for Wilhelm. Sure enough, he is right back in the box on the top of my dresser. I tuck him into my pocket, wondering what he has in store for Beth and Kinsey—the first set of twins, and the next two eldest sisters.

Not surprisingly, I have trouble focusing at work. With each day, each sister, each fantasy, I get closer and closer to being able to give Pippa my name and start a family. I'm having dinner at the palace again tonight and I spend an inordinate amount of time mapping out the castle in my mind for the best places to corner my siren.

Finally, it's after six, and I give up pretending to work. I arrive at the castle and hand my keys off to a valet. I know, not very fitting for an idealistic castle setting, but I'm not going to take a horse and carriage just to indulge you even further in the fantastical aspects of my story. I'll leave it to the fantasies. My world has been turned upside down and inside out enough.

When I enter the house, I can't help but stop and laugh at the sight of Damon crowding Chloe into a corner and kissing her senseless. I give Wilhelm a mental high five and he starts up with his humming again. I'm a little confused at why he's vibrating for them until I notice a movement to my left. I turn my head and another of Pippa's older sisters, Beth, is standing in the doorway of another room smiling fondly at the couple. I look a little closer, and that's when I notice the longing in her eyes.

I think back to my time here as a youth and I don't have many memories of Beth. I do remember her trouble-making twin, Kinsey, though. I only have vague recollections of Beth being there at times, but she was always in the background.

My body snaps tight when the scent of Jasmine fills my nose and blood rushes to my groin at the mere knowledge that Pippa is in the room. I whip around and the moment she sees me, her eyes widen, and her mouth forms a cute little *O*. I'm not even trying to disguise the hunger in my gaze as my eyes scan her from head to toe. In two strides, I'm at her side and crowding her back into the room she just came from. My mouth crashes down on hers, and she melts into me, clinging to my shoulders. After I've had my fill, *for now,* I let her up to breathe. "Fuck, I missed you," I whisper raggedly. She nods absentmindedly, making me smile because she doesn't realize what she's just admitted. Before the fog can clear, I take her hand and lead her back through the castle to the dining hall.

Dinner with the St. Claires is always entertaining. It's rare that, when they get together, it is mother, father, and daughters alone. Instead, it's a loud and fun group of people, but rather than being drawn into the bustle of activity, I find my eyes wandering back to Beth. Her long mahogany hair is braided and pulled over one shoulder, her clothes are not drab, but she doesn't exactly stand out, either. What surprises me most, is that her hazel eyes twinkle with love and merriment as she watches the group and it highlights a beauty people don't seem to notice. Except for Kinsey, who is constantly trying to draw her out. But, Beth continues to watch with amusement, seeming content to stay a wallflower.

With an arm over the back of Pippa's chair, I lean over and ask, "Does Beth have a boyfriend?"

Pippa gives me an arch look. "Looking to trade up so soon? Fantastic." She tries to hide it, but I can hear the disgruntlement in her tone.

I tug on one of her long, chocolate brown locks, wishing I could put her over my knee and spank her sassy little ass. I file that thought away for later because I'm currently in no condition to be even more aroused. "Baby, answer the question."

She shrugs, resting an elbow on the table, her chin propped in her hand as she contemplates her sister. "I don't think so. Beth is the kindest and most loving person, but she's so damn shy. We've all tried to pull her from her shell, but she seems content to stay there. I don't want her to be alone." She turns her head now, her eyes wide and innocent, the little brat. "Perhaps we'll just have to be spinsters together forever."

I roll my eyes and slip my hand down, using two fingers to pinch her bottom. Her expression turns dirty, and she opens her mouth, no doubt about to say something that will definitely earn her a swat on her ripe little ass later.

"Um. We have news," Chloe says loudly, interrupting Pippa and gaining everyone's attention. Over the next hour, I sit back in my seat, observing, knowing the smile on my face is probably growing more triumphant by the minute. Chloe and Damon announce their engagement, followed by Willow and James, making the room erupt in excitement and congratulations. Pippa shifts in her seat uncomfortably, almost falling off as her jaw drops. She throws me a few sideways glances, but otherwise, pretends I'm not there. I simply smile and let it all sink in.

When the jubilation dies down, everyone begins saying

their farewells. I keep my eye on Beth, looking for the right opportunity to slip her the key. Wilhelm seems more interested in her than Kinsey tonight. Finally, as I walk to the front of the castle, I find myself alone with Beth. Lucky me— or maybe it's Wilhelm who makes it happen—she trips and I catch her before she hits the ground. Once she is stable, I lean down to the floor and pick up the key I "let" fall out of my pocket. Yes, ridiculous, but hey, if you had a better option, take it up with Wilhelm.

"Beth," I inquire, extending my hand. "Did you drop this?"

"Nope," she says, examining it curiously. "It's certainly unique, isn't it?"

"Yes," I agree. "I would imagine whomever left it is bound to come back and look for it. Why don't you hang on to it?"

She takes the key with a smile, "Will do. Oh, and Oliver" —she leans in, her voice suddenly a conspiratorial whisper— "let me know if there is anything I can do to help you out with Pippa." She winks, slipping the key into the pocket of her jeans, and with a wave, turns to run up a grand staircase. I chuckle to myself; she's about to help me out tremendously and doesn't even realize it. I mentally salute Wilhelm and wish him good luck.

Another restless night is ahead of me but I cling to the successes Wilhelm has had so far.

Meanwhile...

Beth's Fantasy

I CAN STILL SHOW YOU MY SPECIAL PLACE.

The sultry voice of Adele croons from Beth's phone as she wanders the gardens behind the palace. She hums along and inhales the fresh, spring air, breaking down the floral mixtures and categorizing them in her head. With a bachelor's degree in Horticulture and a master's in Landscape Architecture, it's no surprise this is her favorite place to be.

But, the best part is the special garden she has been growing and caring for since she was ten. It was a little bit hidden, and so the groundskeeper had overlooked it for years, causing it to become overgrown and a complete mess. While exploring one day, she'd found the door to it and after telling her father, he suggested she take on the task of reviving it. He'd recognized the depth of her interest and wanted to encourage her to pursue it.

She'd always been the dreamy one, lost to her imagination, and it fueled her creativity to design landscapes. She consulted with the groundskeeper and local florists, eventually designing a perfect little garden. Over the years, little by little, it was really shaping up. It had also become somewhat of a family project, all of them helping out when needed, but always following her direction.

The garden is surrounded by a fence completely covered in ivy, giving the area a private, peaceful feel. She'd had a beautiful, custom gate made to look like an arched wooden door, to completely enclose it. She had her very own *Secret Garden;* she figured she might as well embrace the story.

It's late, perhaps around midnight, but there are outdoor lamps that gave the space a soft glow. Since she'd refused to disturb the growth within, the lamps were installed outside the walls, high enough to curve over and provide illumination.

Arriving at the door, she pulls it open and meanders inside, shutting it behind her. It feels even more like a magical place tonight, though she isn't sure why. She sits on a stone bench to relax but is startled when an odd vibration comes from her pocket. Digging into her jeans, she removes the key Oliver found in the hallway earlier. When it begins to glow, she stares at it, thinking she should probably be panicking, even as her eyes are drawn to another side of the garden and she sees a new door. *I must be sniffing too much Damiana.* She shrugs, if she's high, she might as well go with it, right?

Almost like a magnetic pull, she can tell the key and the door are connected. Even without that though, it's pretty obvious by the matching carving above the lock. Slipping the key into the hole, she turns it, and the door swings open.

It's definitely not what she expected. The gold and cream foyer is amazing, but it's odd—considering her simple tastes—to find herself imagining such lavishness. Even if she *is* high as a kite. An enormous set of double doors have another matching lock, so she repeats the process and— *Definitely*, she thinks, *definitely stoned*.

She's suddenly walking out onto one of the palaces terraces, this one connecting through several sets of glass French doors to an amazing ballroom which, sadly, almost never gets used. Except, tonight, it's seriously hopping. The room is packed with people, all laughing, dancing, and eating delicious-looking hors d'oeuvres. Parties aren't usually her scene, and she considers returning to her little hidey hole until her mind comes down from the clouds, and then going to bed. She takes a step back, stumbling from her precarious balance, due to the spiked heels she didn't realize she was wearing.

Even with nobody there to witness it, she blushes, realizing these are the shoes she keeps hidden way back in her closet. A guilty pleasure she knew she would never wear wear, but couldn't help indulging in. Skimming her eyes up the rest of her body, she recognizes the shimmery, black mini-skirt, and the red corset top, both having come from that same stash. She'd let a saleswoman talk her into trying the outfit on one day, and when she looked into the mirror, she kind of liked the new version of herself. Particularly the top, it made the girls look fantastic, when they are normally quite . . . well, normal. Beth isn't an ugly duckling suddenly turned into a swan, she isn't plain, or unattractive; she just doesn't stand out. And, most of the time, she is perfectly fine with it. But, in her secret, most personal fantasies, she dreams of being someone people notice. Well, not *people*, just one person. Her soulmate. Whoever he is. So, she bought the outfit, then stuffed it away in her closet, because fantasies are by definition, imagining things that are impossible or improbable. Stepping to the side, she blends into the wall and watches for a few minutes. She is the quintessential wallflower and she always will be.

With a sigh, Beth turns to make her way back through the enchanted door but isn't able to take more than one step before someone grabs her elbow and spins her around. Unused to the heels, and in a state of surprise, she lurches forward into a pair of strong arms, slamming up against a muscular chest. "Oof!"

The arms tighten, and the sexiest voice she has ever heard says, "Leaving so soon?"

If she were wearing panties—*I'm not wearing panties? What the hell? It appears, deep down, I'm quite the hussy*—they would be bursting into flames. Her insides melt and without a barrier to keep it contained, wetness leaks onto her inner thighs.

His blond hair, in need of a cut, ruffles in the evening breeze, and his amazing eyes are surrounded by thick lashes of the same golden color. An angular jaw, high cheek bones, and the fact that he is obviously over six foot, makes her think he must be of Scandinavian heritage. She briefly wonders what their kids would looks like, since they are such opposites in looks. *Whoa there, Nelly. You might want to back up, then back up even more.*

"I, um…" She is already stuttering over her words, then she makes the mistake of looking up and connecting with the most startling blue eyes she's ever seen. *Ever.* As if their beauty alone isn't enough to fluster her, they are filled with heat. Like, I want to rip your panties off (*He doesn't know I'm not wearing panties, right?*) and have my way with you right now, kind of heat.

He loosens his embrace and steps away, only far enough to run his ocean blue orbs over her body, leaving a wake of fire in their path. "I can't let you go anywhere, I'm afraid," he says once his eyes return to hers. His voice is like smooth, rich espresso, jolting her every nerve and making her hypersensitive. She is suddenly grateful for the tight bindings of her top since they keep the world from seeing the way her nipples harden.

"What?" she asks in a high voice. She'd rather we not classify it as a squeak, denial is such a lovely place.

"You're too fucking beautiful. If you leave, someone else might find you, and if they touched you, I'd have to kill them," he growls menacingly.

What exactly are you supposed to say to something like that? Maybe if she wasn't *insanely* attracted to him, she could have had a true feminist moment and slapped his handsome face. Or, been afraid of him, considering the frightening look on his face. Yeah, no. Instead, she swoons and mentally calculates what it would take to get him to take her to a dark corner and fuck her. *Hussy, indeed.*

"What is your name, gorgeous?" he queries, tugging her back into his arms.

"Beth," she says on a gasp, her close proximity to his body making it *very* clear he wants her.

"Beth," he repeats as a smile grows on his face. "I'm Andrew." His face lowers, his lips coming closer and closer to hers, all the while his eyes hold a warning. Somehow, she knows what he's saying with the look; speak now or forever be his. Is this supposed to be a tough question? She closes the gap, pressing her lips against his, giving herself over to him. He groans and uses his thumb to nudge her chin down, opening her mouth so he can plunge his tongue inside. Angling his head, he deepens the kiss and gathers her up in his arms, holding her as close as he can. He starts walking forward, backing her up against the railing of the terrace that overlooks the vast gardens. Gliding his hands from where they'd been caressing her back, down to fill them with her ass. He lifts her, molding their bodies together, and the large bulge in his pants pressing into her heat. Then, he sets her on the railing, spreading her legs so he can stand in between them, before gluing their bodies together again.

She gasps when she feels a finger trailing up her thigh, under her skirt, and running through the lips of her naked pussy. He grunts and dips his finger inside her. "As much as I appreciate the easy access, gorgeous," he mumbles against her lips, "I don't ever want to find you without panties in public, again." He adds a second finger and scissors them, making her moan as her body begins to spiral. "This pussy is all mine, and I don't want even the slightest chance that someone else might see it."

Using his teeth, he tugs down one side of her corset until a breast springs free, then latches on to the nipple. His increases the speed of his fingers—in and out—until her every muscle is frozen to the point of pain. Removing them, he pinches her clit and bites down on her nipple, causing her to splinter apart. Catching her scream with his mouth, he returns his fingers inside to work her slowly down. After a few minutes, he rips his lips away, panting and staring into her eyes with an unreadable emotion. "Exquisite," he whispers gruffly. "I don't know what's happening here, gorgeous. All I know is, from the moment I saw you, you were mine."

She honestly can't argue with his logic, especially when her body is floating to the ground in post orgasmic bliss. Besides, she'd felt the same thing, her body and heart yearning for him instantly. "How did you even see me?" She cocks her head, honestly curious.

Andrew's brows furrow as he looks at her incredulously. "How could I miss you, Beth?"

Helping her off of the railing, he rights her top and smooths down her skirt, before extending his hand towards her. Without hesitation, she takes it and an idea has her tugging it earnestly. "I want to show you something."

He smiles at her enthusiasm and lets her lead the way. She turns towards the door only to find it gone. And with it, the key. Well, fuck a duck. How was she supposed to get back through? In case you were wondering, it was about halfway into her orgasm when she accepted the fact that she wasn't high and this is clearly some sort of alternate universe.

She had every intention of taking him through it with her; she refused to entertain the idea of going back without him.

She'd finally found him—the *one*—her soulmate, and there was no way she was letting him go.

"If you're looking for the door you came in through, I don't think it works like that, gorgeous." Andrew's comment had her whipping around in astonishment and complete confusion. He shrugs, but his expression is frustrated. "I know this isn't reality as much as you do. I just haven't found a solution yet, because I'm not giving you up."

His words do funny things to her stomach and her heart skips a beat. Clutching his hand tightly, she leads him to the stone steps of the terrace and down into the gardens. "I can still show you my special place. My *Secret Garden*."

When they reach the secret garden, he looks around in awe. "This is amazing, Beth."

She blushes and he runs a finger over the pink-tinged cheek. "This is what I do. I'm a landscape architect."

He raises a brow, studying her for a minute, before chuckling. "I should have guessed my perfect woman would work with plants." At her questioning look, he goes on, "I'm a botanist."

Before she can control her mouth, she says, "You're a geek? But, you're so hot." Then, she slaps her hands over her mouth, mortified. Andrew bursts out laughing and scoops her into his arms, planting a hard kiss on her lips.

"Yeah, gorgeous, I'm a complete nerd. I may not look like it, but trust me, inside, I've got the glasses, bow tie, and pocket protector."

Beth giggles and snuggles into him as he settles on one of the wicker chairs situated in the center of the garden. They talk, for what seems like hours, getting to know each other and sneaking in kisses and touches here and there. But, it's late, and as hard as she fights it, eventually, she falls asleep.

∼

Andrew wanders through the palace gardens, following the directions given to him and trying not to get lost. The grounds are incredible, and he can't wait to see this special garden the king had told him about. He'd only recently moved to the country to set up a lab for an in-depth study of the land and how they can increase more productive crops and use plant biology for other resources.

He'd been very curious to meet one of the princesses who is in a similar field, but had yet to make her acquaintance. After showing interest in the garden that was, apparently, her baby, one of her sisters suggested he might find her there. When he spots the door, he can't help laughing at the idealistic picture it creates, transporting you to another time and place. Frances Hodgson Burnett would be proud. The door opens easily, despite its weight, and he steps inside, halting on a gasp. It's the most incredible, magical, unbelievably gorgeous thing he's ever seen. And, the garden is amazing, too.

"You!" a sweet voice exclaims, her hazel eyes blinking at him, mirroring the same astonishment he's feeling. He dreamt about her. This is the woman he spent his night fantasizing about. With this realization, there is an even stronger emotion overriding the surprise. Possessiveness. There is no doubt, in his mind or heart, this woman is meant for him. He strides over to her and lifts her from the chair where she is reading, and his mouth crashes down on hers. Satisfaction roars through him when she melts like butter, and one word pings around in his head like an erratic pinball.

Mine.

Double the trouble

OLIVER

I can't deny the power of love at first sight after meeting Philippa St. Claire. In fact, I'm putting a whole lot of faith in the idea right now. I've never paid much attention to the love lives of other people—until now. So, besides Odette, I really have no clue whether the rest of the St. Claire sisters are in a relationship or not. I don't dwell on it overly much; it's Wilhelm's job to play matchmaker.

Kinsey, Beth's twin, is a fashion designer and up until a few weeks ago, was living in Paris doing an extended internship. I would like to kiss whomever convinced her to move back because getting Wilhelm to her would have been a bitch. As it turns out, we are both attending the same charity function tonight. Pippa is being stubborn, *as usual*, so I'm going stag. I don't much care for these dinners, but I would have enjoyed seeing my girl in a sexy dress. Then again, I don't know if I could have handled all of the other men seeing her like that.

I have to make an appearance and it will give me the chance to slip Kinsey the key before I make an unnoticed exit. It turns out to be easier than I expected. Kinsey isn't the same boisterous, fun-loving girl I remember. She puts on a good front, chatting and smiling but it doesn't reach her eyes.

She spots me and, for once, I see a spark of the old her in those hazel eyes. She hurries over and throws her arms around me in a hug. I stagger back a little, taken off guard by the affectionate action. Wilhelm does his little dance in my pocket. "Hey, Oliver!" she exclaims. "It's good to see you."

My brow lifts, wondering what she's up to. "I don't recall you even knowing I was alive when you were young, Kinsey."

She laughs and looks around, frowning when she doesn't see what she's looking for. "Where's Pippa?"

Ah, now it makes sense. I grin and shake my head. "Were you attempting to make my woman jealous, Kinsey?"

She laughs and shrugs. "Whatever it takes." The light in her eyes dims just slightly. "She shouldn't waste time and risk you giving up and walking away."

Now, that's interesting.

"Never going to happen," I state firmly, my tone leaving zero room for argument.

"Oh, I know. I'm—anyway. She should realize a great thing when she's got it." She pats my cheek and winks. "Good luck, Oliver."

Leaning down, I kiss her cheek, drop the key into her purse, and whisper, "If he let you walk out the door, he was obviously an idiot. Don't lose hope in finding your true love. Someone worthy of you."

I stand back up, and she looks at me inquisitively. "Thanks. How did you know?"

"Lucky guess," I say sympathetically.

"Well, anyway, it really is nice to see you, Oliver." She gives my arm a squeeze, and I lift my chin in farewell before slipping out.

This guy is obviously back in France. I mentally bang my head against a wall and send a telepathic lecture to Wilhelm.

This one is going to be twice as hard to accomplish as Beth's. He'll need to have some kind of unicorn up his sleeve to pull it off.

At home, I hang my tux and then stand there and stare at my closet, feeling restless. Another night of tossing and turning without Pippa doesn't sound appealing. I decide to spend some time clearing space for my love when I finally have her in our home.

Meanwhile...

Kinsey's Fantasy

PRINCE CHARMING WAS A PUSSY

Kinsey stares at herself in the mirror of the ladies room at the banquet hall hosting a charity ball. There was a time when she'd never gone to any kind of function dateless. Before she'd gone to Paris and met Cole, subsequently attending every function alone from then on. He certainly wasn't going to accompany her, and she couldn't bear to go with anyone else.

Mostly, she stopped attending social events at all, but her employer had a lot to do with this charity and since the company was based in Paris, representing them at functions here was one of their stipulations for her moving back to her own country. She is setting up a new fashion house here and works remotely for everything she can, though it will require the occasional trip back.

She loathed the idea of going back and running into Cole. He'd been her supervisor for her internship and, despite working directly under him (if only that pun was intended . . . wishful thinking and all that bullshit), he barely noticed she was alive. No matter how hard she tried, excelling in every task he gave her, wearing the sexiest clothes she could get away with and still be professional, nothing seemed to draw his attention her way. To be fair, no woman had his attention. He was so focused on the job; he was practically blind to the rest of life. The weird thing was, she could have sworn the attraction was mutual.

After the internship was over, she'd taken a permanent position with the company, hoping once he was no longer her supervisor, he'd open his eyes and notice her. The fashion house had already approached her with the idea of expanding to her country and after discussing it with her father, she knew it would do her homeland a lot of good. Still, she put off giving them a final answer until it became abundantly clear— Cole was never going to come around.

So, she left and here she is. Her gown is a silver couture piece (another perk of the job—wearing the clothes). The matching shoes remind her of Cinderella's and she winces as she shifts. It's easy to imagine glass slippers being this uncomfortable, too. She pulls the pins from her bun, allowing her long, mahogany hair to tumble down her back, and sighs. The tension headache forming eases, and she runs her fingers through the strands before deciding it's as good as it's going to get and leaves the bathroom.

As she pulls open the door, something clatters to the floor from her purse. She kneels down and looks around but all she sees is a skeleton key made of gold. It doesn't look familiar, and she isn't sure how it came to be in her purse. She picks it up, noting it weighs at least a pound, making her wonder how she hadn't noticed it in her purse.

Still staring at the key, she walks through the open door, but quickly comes to a halt when she looks up and sees she's in some kind of foyer, judging by the thick gold doors and the lavish, crystal chandelier hanging above her head. She must have gone through the wrong door, although, she could have sworn the bathroom only had one exit. Turning around, she goes to push the door back in but . . . where the fuck did the door go?

Taking deep breathes, Kinsey tries to make sense of what's happening, avoiding the possibility that she might be having a mental breakdown. Figuring the best course of action is to see where the other doors dump her out, she examines them. The key is still clenched in her fist, and as she bends down to look at the lock, she feels it vibrate. Her hand opens and she drops the key as though it had burned her. It lies on the ground, glowing slightly, and she gets the distinct impression that it unlocks the door in front of her. Another deep, calming breath. Picking up the key, she inserts it into the lock and turns. Without provocation, the door glides open, the key still in the lock, and she's staring at the same lobby she'd come from when she entered the bathroom. Bringing two fingers to each temple, she rubs slowly, the tension headache beginning to return.

"Kinsey."

Kinsey freezes at the sound of the voice. *Holy fuck!* Wow, her imagination has clearly started working overtime as if she is hearing Cole's voice when other men speak to her. Except . . . the spicy scent surrounding her is so much like Cole's aftershave. The heat at her back, the goosebumps suddenly all over her body, the butterflies in her belly, the French accent that dissolves her into a puddle of want, they all indicated that if this isn't Cole, it's his doppelgänger.

"Kinsey. *Bébé.*"

Did he just call me baby? Seriously. *What. The. Fuck?* Kinsey spins around and glares at the beautiful man who never failed to make her weak in the knees. And, it really, really isn't fair that she seems to be the only one on the verge of spontaneously combusting from lust when they are around each other. This time, though, the hurt and anger are strong enough to help her keep her composure. Otherwise, she might have simply melted, and how embarrassing would that have been?

"Cole." Her voice doesn't waiver, coming across emotionless, and she barely restrains a fist pump in victory. Maybe she will actually walk away with her dignity intact. Only in her dreams has she ever been able to keep her composure around Cole. "What are you doing here?"

He looks so much the same—tall, lean, and curly brown hair. Heartbreakingly handsome. His brown eyes, framed by long, black lashes, pierce through her, and she fights the temptation to squirm. She always felt like he could see inside her and wondered how it was he could ignore the burning passion and love she had for him. There is something in his gaze she's never seen before. Or, a more apt description might be that she can see everything in his eyes, as though he's removed walls she hadn't been able to see past before. And, what she sees is freaking her the fuck out.

"I'm here for you, Kinsey." His velvety voice is almost her undoing. He prowls closer and Kinsey backs up, desperately trying to keep distance between them. There is hunger is his gaze; he's staring at her like she is his next meal.

Shaking her head, she puts a hand out to stop his advance. "*Arrêtez*," she begs raggedly.

"*Non, bébé*," he answers with a scowl.

One more step back and Kinsey bumps into another body. "Sorry!" she apologizes as she tries to catch her balance. There is a bit of a shuffle and Kinsey seizes the opportunity to take off in the crowd. To her shock, she's in the middle of the same ballroom, but everything is different. The room is lit by oil sconces; the women are dressed in large, fairytale-type ball gowns, while the men are dressed much as the princes are in the same stories. They are dancing the waltz, spinning around the room, and suddenly she's being swept away in the same dizzying pattern.

Cole holds her close as he leads, swirling and stepping in time to the music. Kinsey looks up in confusion, not understanding what's happening. His face is soft and tender as he gazes down at her, and when he bends his head to brush his lips over hers, it leaves a delicious tingle behind. "*Si belle*," he murmurs. *He thinks I'm beautiful?* Her valiant attempts to stay unaffected are failing miserably and she feels hope lift her heart.

It seems as though the whole world fades away, including the ballroom where they are dancing. Kinsey looks down and sees nothing but clouds at their feet. Cloud nine? Somebody is having too much fun with the realism of expressions...

Finally, the floor solidifies under their feet again and they stop spinning. Keeping her hand firmly clasped in his, he leads her out the front door to the relative quiet of the night. He stops once they are out of the way from people leaving the party and leans against a wall. With his hands on her hips, he situates her so she is standing between his legs.

"I don't understand what's happening," she cries softly.

"*Je suis désolé mon amour.*" His voice breaks slightly as he apologizes, running a hand over her hair and kissing her forehead. "I should never have let you go. I won't make the same mistake twice."

"Why?" Tears are making tracks down her cheeks, and he wipes them away with his thumbs before framing her face in his big hands.

"Because, I'm a fucking idiot, *bébé*," he admits. Kinsey sniffs and nods her agreement, making him chuckle. "When you first arrived, I was blown away by my . . . *envie* . . . desire, for you," he says, struggling a tiny bit with his English. Of course, the more he speaks in French, the more of her resistance fades away. "I couldn't do anything about it while you were working for me. So, I did my best to . . .eh. . .*voir tout sauf vous* . . . focus on other things, I guess?" He raises a brow to ask if she's following. Kinsey speaks fluent French, but she doesn't remind him of this, preferring to make him work for it. "Then, you were gone and *merde, bébé*, my life fell apart."

"Really?" Kinsey sniffs.

"Really," he affirms.

"What if I've moved on?" she asks hesitantly.

His face darkens, his brown eyes becoming fierce and he growls, "*Tu es à moi, bébé.*"

Swoon. Kinsey takes a step back, not ready to give into this dream; it will only hurt so much more when she wakes. She needs time to think, to process what the hell is happening. Lifting the hem of her dress, she skips down the steps as quickly as she can without tripping in her ridiculous heels.

"Kinsey!" His footfalls are right behind her and she knows she can't outrun him. Huffing in annoyance, she stops and kicks her shoes off before sprinting the rest of the way to the bottom. It's well after midnight, so it's not like a pumpkin carriage is going to show up, but luck is with her because there happens to be an orange cab. *Wait, what century are we in again?*

She doesn't know how, but she manages to elude Cole before diving into the back seat of the vehicle. But then, Cinderella out ran Prince Charming (although, I think we can all agree on what a pussy he was), so I guess this shoeless maiden can do the same.

The cab speeds off, and she gives him her address, then slumps back, contemplating her circumstances. When the car finally pulls up the curb in front of her house, she spots a white Knight XV in the driveway. She rolls her eyes. *This is getting out of hand.* After paying the driver, she hops out and traipses across her front yard, no longer trying to outrun him. Still, she jumps when the driver's side door slams and Cole rounds the car, calm as can be.

She stops at her front door and faces him. "How did you know where to find me?"

Cole answers as he strides purposefully towards her. "Perhaps I spoke with your ... eh, mère fée"—he stops and chews on his lip for a second, thinking, then seems to settle on a phrase— "fairy mother?" He smiles at his little joke, but Kinsey is not amused and continues to stare at him.

He pouts for a moment, then shrugs. "I called your parents." Standing in front of her now, he twists the knob on her door and it opens, without the key. He puts his hand on her lower back and guides her inside. The door shuts, and he sweeps her into his arms, carrying her to a couch in the first room he comes across. Taking a seat, he settles her in his lap, and Kinsey feels all of the resistance melt away. The truth is, she loves him and is happy he's here. His arms wrap around her, and she snuggles down into his embrace, taking a deep inhale of his spicy scent. "I've asked to be part of the team getting the fashion house off the ground," he informs her.

Kinsey's nose wrinkles, not liking this at all. "You're going to be my boss, again? But—"

"Didn't you know this position was a—pro—eh, promotion?" he asks, clearly surprised. She sits up and faces him, her jaw hanging down, and shakes her head. Cole laughs and gives her a quick, hard kiss. "We are equals, bébé. Partners."

"Seriously?" Kinsey practically shouts with excitement.

"Oui, bébé," he whispers before kissing her again, this time slow and deep, exploring her mouth with his tongue, and causing the butterflies in her stomach to party like it's Mardi Gras. "I love you, Kinsey. I will go wherever you are." The words are mumbled against her lips.

Kinsey disengages her mouth and rears back to be able to look him in the eyes. The sincerity she finds on his face is her undoing. "I love you too, Cole."

He grins, and she could swear his chest literally puffs up a little with pride and it makes her giggle. Cupping her face between his hands, he sweetly kisses her forehead, eyelids, nose, and lastly, her mouth. "You have three months, bébé." Kinsey's brows lower as she tries to figure out what he's talking about. He winks, his grin back in place on his perfect face. "To plan our wedding."

There is only a moment of hesitation before Kinsey decides to say fuck it and throws rationality out the window. "Three months, then," she agrees. His expression of joy lights up the world around her and she could swear something akin to magic is crackling in the air.

Cole holds her to him as he stands, raising a brow in question. Kinsey laughs and directs him to the bedroom. He takes his time with her, savoring and loving on her body, leaving no spot untouched. When they are both naked and pressed together, desperate for completion, he pushes up on his elbows and looks down at her. "Birth control?" he asks.

She cringes. "No, and I don't have any condoms, either."

He jerks his head up and down once, his face determined as he says, "Good. I want to see you with a round belly, growing a little one made of you and me." He narrows his eyes, daring her to object. "No protection, bébé. I'm going to give you my baby."

Once again, Kinsey vaguely wonders if she should be thinking this over, but ultimately, it's what she wants. "Knock yourself out." She laughs at his puzzled expression. "It means, go for it. Yes." With no more preamble, he thrusts inside, and it isn't long before they're both flying high, right back on the cloud they'd been dancing on.

~

Cole runs a hand through his hair nervously. He knows convincing Kinsey he loves her is going to be an uphill battle but he puts on some proverbial armor and readies himself for the fight. He knocks on the door of the house and waits, hoping he got the address her sister had given him correct.

When it opens, an adorably mussed, sleepy-eyed Kinsey stands in front of him. She looks bewildered for a moment, then the morning fog starts to clear as her eyes widen. Before he can open his mouth to give her his perfectly rehearsed speech, she grabs his shirt and yanks, causing him to stumble into the house. Twisting the fabric in clenched fists, she glares at him. "You better be here to tell me you love me and are moving to Rêves to be with me."

Cole's eyebrows shoot sky high, his face a mask of disbelief, warring with hope, and he can only manage a nod. Her face softens with a smile. "You can grovel later, right now, I just want to be with you." She takes his hand, and he follows blindly behind her, until they reach a bedroom. *If this is a dream*, he thinks, *please don't ever let me wake up.*

Forcing might be a bit of a stretch

PIPPA

My sister Kinsey called today. I ignored the sneaky suspicion about why she was calling, until my mother started squawking and clapping, evidently thrilled with whatever Kinsey had to say. The guy she'd been pining over had shown up, and they were engaged. *Engaged!*

It was just my luck that Oliver happened to be there when the call came.

I eye him suspiciously, trying not to laugh when he winks and wiggles his eyebrows. He holds up seven fingers with an arrogant grin, and I blanch. Was this his doing? No, that's crazy, right? How could he possibly be orchestrating my sisters' love lives? I shake the absurd thought out of my head.

I am easily distracted when he stands, his back muscles rippling and his spectacular ass on display. It certainly doesn't help that I'm still tingling from when he'd hauled me over to his side, forcing me to cuddle up to his warm, delicious body. I do a mental face plant into the cushions, I have to stop ogling him or pretty soon, the side of me that likes the idea of being tied to this sexy man will win.

Jealous of a cupcake

OLIVER

I turn around and catch Pippa's sable eyes on my ass, and her face pinkens with a pretty blush. Eventually, I'm going to discover how far down that pretty pink color goes.

I'd stopped by to spend some time with her and found her reading in the library, so I dropped down next to her, dragged her into my side, and poured over some business contracts. I could see her debating whether to fight me, then she seemed to accept the inevitable and relaxed in my hold.

Wilhelm is getting antsy, but I'm not quite sure what to do. Pippa's sister, Jenna, is the oldest of the available sisters now. She lives here at the castle, and I'd hoped to catch her when she came home from work. However, she recently opened The Fairest Cupcake, a bakery situated in the town square of a little village not far from here. Considering what it took to get my own business off the ground in Rêves, I suppose should have expected her to be in the same rabbit hole I'd recently climbed out of.

Dessert suddenly sounds like a fantastic idea. "Let's go and get some of your sister's cupcakes, baby," I suggest and hold my hand out to help her up. Pippa is an absolute sucker for sweets and she, more than anyone, has helped Jenna to get her store running. She licks her lips in anticipation, and I stifle a groan, envious of her tongue. Pippa is more delicious than anything I've ever tasted.

She takes my proffered hand, and I pull her to her feet, suppressing the instinct to throw her over my shoulder and run away with her. I'm pleasantly surprised when she continues to hold my hand, allowing me to guide her out to my car, and get her seated and belted in. I get into the car and lace my fingers with hers, resting our hands on my thigh.

The drive to The Fairest Cupcake doesn't take long, and when we walk inside, we see Jenna behind the counter, serving a line of customers. Like the others, Jenna is quite obviously Pippa's sister, but she's also drastically different. Her eyes are a dark, emerald green, and her hair is almost black. She wears it in a short style, the curls ending just below her ears. Her skin is much paler, and I've rarely seen her without her blood-red lipstick.

The line dies down and she notices us, rushing over to hug us both. "I tried something new today, you guys are going to be my guinea pigs," she announces, dragging us to a different table than the one we'd settled at. She goes back behind the counter and gets into the glass display case by the register. There are two cupcakes on the plate she's holding when she returns, both covered in a red glaze to make the cake look like a shiny apple, there is even a chocolate "stem" sticking out of the top. Pippa's musical laugh brings a smile to my face, and I wait, content to watch her as she bites into the confection. Her eyes roll and she moans, forcing me to concentrate on the cupcake instead of her, attempting to get my dick to settle back down.

"Jenna, it's amazing," Pippa mumbles around a mouth full of the tasty treat. "I'm having a foodgasm over here." I frown, irrationally pissed that something, *anything*, besides me is giving her any kind of orgasmic pleasure. Jenna claps and bounces excitedly, turning to me. I bite into the apple-flavored dessert, and Pippa is right, it's incredible. Even though I know it's cake, I could swear my mouth filled with apple juice. I nod at her, too busy devouring my cupcake to form words. Jenna laughs and does a fist pump in the air.

The bell over the door rings and Jenna's face immediately flushes. Glancing over, I see a blond-haired man entering, his eyes straying instantly to Jenna. *Well, well, isn't this interesting?* Wilhelm begins his little cha-cha cha in my pocket, and I peek at Pippa to see if she's paying attention. Her head is swiveling back and forth between Jenna and the man, who seemed to be locked into a stare down. I covertly remove Wilhelm from the pocket of my pants and slide it into her apron, hoping she is too distracted to notice the added weight until later.

It seems like an eternity until these two break their connection and, without a word, Jenna heads back to the front of the store, then disappears into the back. The man's face falls and he walks dejectedly to the register and puts in his order. He finally leaves, and we aren't far behind, not having seen Jenna since she scurried into the back of the bakery.

After dropping Pippa off at home and leaving her with swollen lips and a dazed expression, I go to bed and spend another night fantasizing about Pippa, counting the hours until all eleven sisters are paired off.

Meanwhile...

Jenna's Fantasy

YOUR...CUPCAKES ARE SPECTACULAR

"You can go home, sleepy head," Jenna tells her bus boy. He is one of seven brothers she rotates through for odd jobs in the bakery. Today was crazy busy, and she can plainly see he is dead on his feet.

"Okay, thanks, boss," he calls as he trudges out the door. She would be worried about him leaving, being so tired, but the boys live in a rented house that's only a two-minute walk away.

Wiping down the last of her appliances, Jenna steps back and admires her kitchen. She'd admit to having a little help from her parents to get started, but she'd worked her hind end off to do as much on her own as possible. And, she was damn proud. She spies her apron in a heap on one of the counters and goes over to shake it out and hang it up. One of the front pockets seems to have something in it and she sticks two fingers in to lift it out. It looks like a very strange key. It must belong to a customer but, how did it get into her pocket? She studies it absentmindedly while she moseys to her office, intent on putting it in the lost and found. Opening the door, she walks inside and after a few more steps, she runs right into a solid wall. "Motherfucker!" she grunts, putting a hand to her head and feeling a bump already forming. Looking around, she forgets all about her head. She's in a foyer—a great, big, ornate, room—and it isn't a wall she's walked into, it's a tall set of golden, double doors. Freaked, she rushes to return to the door she came through but, it's a solid wall with gold swirled and cream paper.

It's then she remembers the skeleton key, particularly because it's vibrating in her hand and . . . um, glowing? Looking at the door once more, Jenna sees a small carving above the lock; a replica of the item in her hand. Without any other options in sight, she timidly inserts the key into the designated slot and rotates it until she hears a click.

Both doors fly open, banging against the walls on either side, making her flinch. The scene before her has her jaw dropping to the ground and forgetting all about the key. It's a bakery. Her bakery. Well, sort of. It's likely what her bakery would look like if it were being depicted in a fairytale. The setup is the same, with a counter and glass case up front, and tables and chairs throughout. Except, the tables are crudely carved, there is no register, the boy at the counter counts out coins from a bag, and the room it bathed in dim light from lanterns scattered about.

Everyone is dressed in clothes that remind her of the sixteenth century and when she peeks down at her own clothes, they are a similar style. A sweeping, white skirt, a deep blue, boned top with a deep V down the center of her skirt, and blue puffed sleeved attached at her shoulders. *How hard did I hit my head*? It's incredibly busy and a fast inspection of the room reveals all seven of the young brothers are working. One of them is at the register and he seems to notice her all of the sudden and he waves her over.

"Jenna, I'm so glad you're here. The delivery of apples just arrived and it's not our usual supplier. I was afraid to accept it without consulting you."

"I'll check it out," I murmur dazedly and walk to the exit in the back that lets out into an alley. A horse and cart stand, seemingly unattended, and on the side board is a logo; a large apple and the words *Magic Wishing Apples*.

An older woman with long, grey hair, a large nose, and a cigarette between her lips, slinks from around the corner, startling Jenna. She scowls in irritation. "Where is Ted?" she snaps. "And, please don't smoke here. We deal with food, for crying out loud."

The woman shrugs and drops it to the ground, crushing it under her boot. Jenna holds in a biting remark figuring it isn't worth the effort. She'd call Ted, oh wait—no phones. Um, she'd send him a message, and find out who the hell this is and make sure she is never sent to The Fairest Cupcake again.

"Ted's out sick, asked me to make the drop today." She grins and it doesn't do her looks any favors, especially the yellowing teeth. "Besides, these are the best apples you'll ever get. Wait till you taste one, dearie."

This was definitely getting weirder by the minute and there was something familiar about it all. Either way, she needed the inventory, and if Ted had sent the woman, Jenna trusted his judgment enough to accept the delivery. Once the boys have the fruit all unloaded, the woman hauls herself up onto the horse and with one last, very odd, look, she drives the cart off into the night.

Shaking it off, Jenna returns to the front of the store and stops short when she sees an incredibly handsome, blond man ordering at the counter. As though there were a magnetic force between them, his head flips in her direction, and they stare at each other. Heat engulfs her body as his dark, almost grey, eyes survey her. Damn, he's sexy. His bottom lip is slightly bigger than the top, and she would love nothing more than to bite it. However, in the three months that he has been a daily customer, she's never worked up the courage to approach him. Every day he doesn't make a move, she is more and more convinced he doesn't feel the same level of attraction and talks herself out of acting on it.

She almost faints when, for the first time, he walks in her direction. Her heart beats so hard, she is sure he can hear it. The heat she feels inside is burning her skin, making it clear to her that she is blushing from head to toe.

He doesn't stop until he is directly in front of her, closing the gap between them, ignoring the rules of personal space. Not that she minds. In fact, in her opinion, he's still not close enough. "Jenna." She shivers at the gritty sound of his voice. She hadn't thought he could get any sexier. *Wrong.* "I'm Hunter." *Double wrong.*

"Hi," she squeaks out in a higher voice than normal. She clears her throat and tries again. "Hi, um, nice to meet you."

He cocks his head to the side, observing her with a small smile. "Would you, I mean, could we talk somewhere in private?"

Jenna nods dumbly and leads the way to her office, but halts at the closed door. The last time she stepped through this door, it took her here, and she isn't about to leave now that she and Hunter are finally moving forward. She could open it and simply not step through, right? Would Hunter find that weird? She sighs and slowly cracks the door. It leads to her office. She blows out a breath of relief and goes inside. Here, too, everything is similar and yet, different in style and age.

With no warning, she finds herself being whirled around and molded to Hunter's hard body. Her breasts press against his defined chest and her nipples harden, her hands landing on his muscular biceps. The bulge digging into her stomach makes her very aware of what her proximity is doing to him.

He isn't overly bulky, and his build doesn't seem gym

grown; she wonders what he does for a living, assuming whatever it is attributes to his fantastic body. His grey eyes are like molten silver as he drinks in the sight of her, lingering hungrily on her lips.

"I've waited far too long to taste you," he growls before covering her mouth with his own. Jenna is in complete agreement and throws herself into the kiss with gusto. When his head rears back and he looks at her, his gaze is unreadable, and she wonders if she came on too strong. *There goes the blushing again,* she groans to herself. Her worries are set aside when he flashes a big smile and dives back in, devouring her mouth, his hands finding her butt cheeks and lifting her against him. He tears his lips away only long enough to spot a chair and swiftly walks to it. He sits and lifts Jenna's skirt so it bunches around her waist, making a noise of frustration at the amount of fabric between them. *This time period doesn't seem very conducive to quickies.* Spreading her legs, he settles her on his lap so she is straddling him. He is big *everywhere,* and she can feel his rock hard cock against her pussy, making her squirm. He grips her hips to keep her still. "Don't move like that, sweetheart, or I won't be able to control myself," he says with a groan.

"Why . . . now?" she asks, panting, her heart racing, and her body electrified like live wires.

"I don't know," he claims. "I've wanted you for so long and today I finally gathered the courage to go after you." His hands slowly travel from her hips, up her torso, to cup her full breasts. "Now, I know I won't ever let you go." He dips a finger inside her low neckline and brushes it over a stiff nipple. She gasps and wiggles again, rubbing herself against him, seeking relief. He growls and flexes his hands on her breasts before tugging her fairly inflexible top until they pop out, the rigid neckline holding them up and together. Hunter's eyes flare and he buries his face between them for a second before wrapping his lips around one peak.

Sparks fly from where he sucks and nips straight to the ache between her legs. He switches sides, and she begins to rock, sliding her pussy over his cock, moaning at the incredible pleasure. He lets her nipple go with a pop and cradles her face in his hands. "I must be crazy, but in my heart, my soul, I know I love you. You are the only one for me."

Jenna stills at his words, her heart soaring, and takes a deep breath, trying to control her craving to move. She turns her face and kisses one of his palms. "Me, too," she whispers. Hunter urges her head forward and takes her mouth in a deep, soul-binding kiss.

"It's too soon. Fuck, I know this is too fast, but damn, Jenna, I *need* to be inside you." His emphasis on need is her undoing and she scoots back on his lap, shoving her skirts out of the way to gain access to his—she's relieved to see pants instead of tights. Wrong era, but she wasn't sure she would have been able to keep from laughing. Mood killer, anyone? He holds the fabric away while she unbuttons him and takes out his long, thick cock. *Hmmm. Impressive.*

Hunter raises her up, and she aligns his member with her pussy before helping her sink down on him. He groans in bliss as he's gloved in her tight, wet heat. "Fuck, sweetheart. You feel perfect. Like you were made for me."

Jenna moans, her heart melting at his declaration. She grabs onto his shoulders for leverage and begins to move up and down, swiveling her hips every once in a while. Her breasts bounce in Hunter's face and he takes full advantage, sucking hard on her nipples, shooting streaks of pleasure down to her pussy, and she cries out. He thrusts up in time with her, their bodies synched in a steady rhythm until he seems to snap. Gripping her hips roughly, he begins to pick her up and slam her back down, getting more frantic with each plunge of his cock inside her.

"Oh, yes! Fuck! Hold me in, sweetheart," he demands, his eyes locked with hers and Jenna bears down every time he elevates her, so his cock drags against her walls. "Just like that, Jenna. Fuck, yes!" She begins to tremble from head to toe, her orgasm building in a swift crescendo. "You're almost there aren't you, sweetheart?" he grunts.

"Yes! Oh, Hunter! Oh, yes!"

"I can feel you coating my cock in your cream, Jenna. Come," he instructs her through gritted teeth, then he seems to really lose it and shouts, "Now!"

Jenna throws her head back and screams his name as her orgasm erupts in a deafening roar, the symphony of sensations creating a Heaven on Earth. Hunter thrusts up hard two more times and on the third, he buries himself as fucking deep as he can and roars his release.

After righting themselves and cleaning up, a task that took much longer due to their need to stop frequently to kiss and caress each other, they walk hand in hand to the door. Reality hits Jenna in the face and she gasps in mortification. The walls are not thick here and where the bakery was full of activity when they slipped into the office, she hears nothing now. Did the sounds of them fucking shock them all into silence? Jenna fervently wishes for a nice, dark hole to open up in the ground and swallow her.

Hunter chuckles and she glares at him until he points to her left and her gaze follows the direction of his finger. A clock shows the time as two in the morning. She hadn't even thought about the fact that her bakery had been hopping well after midnight until this moment. Considering she closes at eight, she shrugs; this is the least weird thing about her night at this point.

Outside the small office, they find the place deserted and

closed up for the night. Jenna finds a note from one of the boys, informing her they'd done all the nightly rituals for closing and she could take off and relax. The P.S. at the bottom makes her smile. They'd used the batch of new apples to make some cupcakes and left a couple of them on the kitchen counter for her.

Grinning, she grabs Hunter's hand and leads the way to the kitchen. "You've got to try these cupcakes." She hears a snicker behind her and peers over her shoulder to see his hungry gaze roving all over her body. Her muscles tighten in anticipation with the memories of what happened last time he looked at her like she was his next meal.

"Sweetheart, I've already tried your cupcakes, and they are spectacular."

Jenna laughs, shaking her head. "Terrible, Hunter. Just terrible. I hope this isn't indicative of your sense of humor and that you're just tired." Finding the container of sweet treats, Jenna lifts the lid and hands one to Hunter. The other cupcake has a note saying the apple lady had told them to make her something special with an apple she insisted was the best of the bushel.

She lifts the cupcake but stops to watch Hunter, and he moans in delight. He leans in and kisses her. "Delicious."

Giggling she asks, "Me or the cupcake?"

Hunter leers at her suggestively. "I think that theory can only be truly tested by putting them together. I'll have to eat some of these off of you, sweetheart."

Her whole body tingles and she can't help the wide smile plastered on her face. Bringing the dessert to her mouth, she takes a bite and the world goes dark.

~

Hunter bangs on the back door of The Fairest Cupcake. He can't explain it, but he woke in a cold sweat this morning, worry for Jenna coursing through his veins. He'd spent the night fantasizing about finding the courage to finally take her and make her his. He'd never been a coward in his life, but the world tilted on its axis around Jenna, gripping him in fear because he knew, if she rejected him, he'd more than likely kidnap her and take her somewhere to seduce her until she changed her mind. His dream had seemed unbelievably real and he'd actually come all over himself from merely imagining fucking Jenna.

After a minute he stops pounding and looks at the door handle, wondering if he should try it. Making up his mind, he twists the knob and is equal parts relieved to be getting inside and pissed that Jenna has left herself unprotected.

It's five in the morning, and he knows she is usually here prepping for the day. It's likely she's alone and he doesn't want to scare her, so he calls her name immediately. There is no answer so he goes further inside until he enters the kitchen. His blood turns to ice at the sight of Jenna sprawled on the floor, eyes closed, and her skin paler than usual. He rushes over and kneels at her side, bending over to clear her tangled hair away from her face.

Her pouty lips are still painted red from her lipstick and before he is able to check himself, he leans down and presses his lips to hers. When she moans, he breathes a sigh of relief and peppers her whole face with kisses.

"Hunter?" she mumbles. Her eyes are still closed and his heart starts beating rapidly. How does she know his name? Blinking lethargically and looking around, her emerald green eyes come to rest on his face, and she smiles softly. "Hey, did we pass out on a sugar and sex high?"

"A what?" he croaks.

Her eyes skim down his body and then they widen with

mortification as her skin flushes red. She sits and scrambles backward in a crab crawl. "I didn't—I mean, just ignore me. Sorry. I thought you were someone else. Forget I said anything. Have you had breakfast? Although, I wouldn't suggest anything apple," she rambles nervously.

Apples? It's not possible, is it? "Jenna, Jenna, calm down, sweetheart," he soothes. She looks at him oddly, and he knows she's got the same questions running through her mind. "Did you dream about me last night?"

Her blush deepens and she looks everywhere but at him. "Um . . . why would—I don't even know you—"

"—I dreamt about you," he cuts her off, deciding to not beat around the bush. She looks at him again, still blushing adorably, but noticeably curious. "I dreamt that I finally manned up and came after you. I made you mine, like you're are meant to be."

Her mouth forms a little *O*, and he nods to punctuate his statement. Might as well be blunt and to the point; it is what it is. She is his and the sooner she figures it out, the sooner he can make his dream a reality.

"Does that mean you're mine?" she asks shyly.

"Completely," he confirms and crawls over to where she's backed herself against the wall. He pulls her into his arms and takes her spot on the floor.

"Deal," she says confidently and he can't stop himself from kissing her, repeatedly, until they break apart to take in great gulps of air.

Staring at the floor, he remembers how he found her and frowns. "Sweetheart, why were you passed out on the floor?"

She thinks for a minute then shrugs. "I have no idea. But, I have no problem with you making a habit of kissing me awake."

He chuckles and gathers her a little closer. "Every day, for the rest of your life, sweetheart."

If the shrew fits

OLIVER

Wilhelm is back in his box this morning, like he has been every morning. And yet, I exhale a sharp breath in relief, afraid that this is all too good to be true. My dreams of Pippa at night are making it harder and harder (no pun intended) to wake up without her. If things keep on schedule, I have six more nights. Six nights until she is all mine. Forever.

I get ready for the day and head to my office, throwing myself into the mounds of paperwork on my desk. My door is mostly left open so I am accessible to my employees without them having to go through a gatekeeper. Although, it seems I've been a lot less approachable lately, or so Simon tells me. *The little bastard*. I should point out that he's been just as much of a grouch lately, but I don't need the added grief it would be sure to bring me. On days like today, when I am behind and not in the mood to deal with bullshit, I shut the door and instruct Abbi to keep everyone out. Except Pippa, of course.

The morning is productive and it relieves some of my stress, not to mention that it helps distract me from my growing need for Pippa. I'm in a much better mood when Abbi buzzes me at one in the afternoon and tells me Iris is here to see me. I'm curious as to what she needs from me considering she isn't my employee. She is a highly sought-after art expert, specializing in rare books. Wilhelm chooses this instant to start putting up a racket, and I realize why, remembering that the twins, Iris and Piper, are the next two sisters down the line. It must be Iris's special night. I tell Abbi to send her in and greet her with a warm smile when she enters my office, carrying a box of books. "Iris, what can I do for you?"

She smiles, setting the box on my desk, taking out four of them, and placing them in front of me. She perches on the arm of a chair, flicking her straight, honey-brown hair over her shoulder and brushing her bangs off of her forehead. Though her eyes are a green so light, they are almost translucent, she still bears the St. Claire nose, mouth, and shape of the eyes. Not for the first time, I wonder if my and Pippa's children will carry the dominant features of the royal family. Picturing a sweet baby girl, who looks exactly like her mama, never fails to strengthen my determination to marry my Pippa and knock her the fuck up as soon as possible.

"I found these books in an old section of the library at Vianden Castle when I was in Luxemburg last month. I've been meaning to drop them by."

My brow furrows in confusion and Iris laughs. She gestures to the stack and gives me a scheming smile. "Those are first editions of Pippa's favorite classic novels."

I'm a little taken back by the thoughtful gesture. "Thank you, Iris. These are incredible." I silently give Wilhelm props for this plan, grateful these eleven ladies are getting their happily ever afters.

She sighs and stands. "I'm off to work. The rest of these

were requested to complete a collection in a library I'm going to catalogue." She reaches for the box of books, but before she can lift it, I quickly grab it. "Let me help you," I suggest. She nods her thanks, and I follow her to the parking lot and set the box in the trunk. Just before I close it, I toss Wilhelm in with the books.

Iris is watching me when I straighten back up. "You're good for her," she muses.

"So you've all been telling me," I respond dryly. "Now, if only I could get Pippa to admit she agrees with this opinion."

"She will," she divulges. "Pippa has always maintained that she wouldn't marry until later in life. And then, you come along and upset the balance. All of the sudden, she wants things she'd convinced herself that she didn't. You and I both know; no one is more stubborn than Pippa."

I shake my head in exasperation. "You're right, with one exception," I inform her.

A smile plays around the corners of her mouth and her eyes twinkle. "Why do you think we're rooting for you? If anyone can tame the shrew, it's you, Petruchio." She laughs and opens the driver's door, giving me a wave as she gets in, then drives away.

Returning to my office, I look through the books and find *The Scarlet Pimpernel, Pride & Prejudice, Little Women*, & *Jane Eyre*. All four novels are about strong, independent, courageous women, but I wonder if Pippa realizes that in the end, they each settled down as wives and mothers, having found men who treasured those qualities rather than stifling them. I chuckle at Iris's joking comparison to the Shakespeare play. No, Pippa isn't a shrew, she's full of fire and it's one of the things I love most about her. I don't want to tame her; I simply want her to be mine.

When I get home, I change and head down to my den,

light a fire, and pour myself a drink. I stare into the flames and brood. Every moment I'm not with her, I miss her.

Meanwhile...

Iris's Fantasy

STUCK WITH MR. SEXY MCGROWL? YES, PLEASE

Iris walks up the front steps of the old castle, holding the heavy box of books precariously in her arms. Apparently, it used to belong to a Duke or something, but now it's owned by some mysterious guy nobody knows much about. At the top, she glares at the doorbell, wondering who the hell still had a pull-down ringer? Without available hands, she stares at it, hoping The Force or a magic fairy will ring it for her. She's not about to set this precious box of books on the ground; who knows what could happen. Sighing, she presses the box against the door, bringing up her knee to help support it so she can free up one limb.

Never attempt a career in the circus, your balance sucks. Finally, she's as stable as she's going to get, so she gingerly removes a hand and reaches up towards the handle—fa-thud! When the door suddenly swings open, Iris goes flying forward and lands hard on the floor. The box of books is heavy and the stupid thing simply falls to the ground, completely unharmed.

"Oh! I'm so sorry!"

Iris winces as she crawls to her knees and looks up at the owner of the apologetic voice. An older woman, probably the housekeeper, since the owner is single, holds out her hand to help Iris up.

"Thank you," she says as she grasps the proffered hand.

"No need to be sorry. It wasn't anyone's fault," she assures her with a smile. Once she's on her feet, she squats down to try and lift the books back up. Getting leverage under the heavy box is much harder when it's not elevated, and she blows out a breath in frustration. The woman goes to the opposite side and they attempt is together, successfully hefting it up after a few tries.

"You must be Iris," the woman guesses, her countenance cheerful and welcoming. Having only dealt with the grumpy owner of the castle on the phone, Iris perks up at the pleasant reception. The woman is short and plump, rounder around her middle than anywhere else, with graying hair, pulled into a soft bun, curly strands escaping around her face. "I'm the housekeeper, Mrs. Kettle."

Iris barely suppresses a snort of laughter as her mind conjures up images of talking tea pots. "Yes, I'm Iris," she manages to say with a straight face.

"Great!" Mrs. Kettle (stop laughing!) beams. "Follow me and I'll take you to the library."

They traverse through several halls, turning here and there, until they reach a set of elaborately carved, wooden doors, stretched from floor to ceiling. Mrs. Kettle turns the knob and to Iris's surprise, the heavy door opens smoothly and silently. She crosses the threshold and comes to a standstill, taking in the majestic library with awe. The ceiling rises up at least two stories, and three of the four walls are floor-to-ceiling bookshelves, with a catwalk splitting them in half, reached by a single spiral staircase to the right of the entrance. The fourth wall is completely made of tall, narrow windows with comfortable couches and chairs in front of them, creating little "conversation nooks."

Mrs. Kettle chuckles. "I had the same reaction the first time I visited this room."

Iris finally regains her faculties and sets the box on the nearest sturdy surface, with a grunt.

"There is an intercom system installed," Mrs. Kettle explains and points to a small panel on the wall next to the door. *They installed an intercom but haven't upgraded the doorbell?* Iris mentally rolls her eyes at the thought.

"If you need anything, I'll be in my office, near the kitchens. Don't hesitate to call me." She hands Iris a key and adds, "Here is a key to a side door." She points to an exit directly behind the stairs that Iris hadn't noticed at first. "Come and go to the library as you like, I know this will be a time-consuming project."

"Thank you," Iris says gratefully. Mrs. Kettle smiles brightly and nods before leaving the way she came. Looking around, Iris analyzes the structure of the room and breaks it into chunks, deciding to tackle it from left to right, working her way through until it's done. This job is going to take weeks and weeks to accomplish, but it's what she does and she can't help being excited about it. Grabbing paperwork and her tablet from the box, she sets to work.

Iris is so engrossed in her tasks, she doesn't notice how late it is once she calls it quits. Standing from where she is hunched over on a table doing paperwork, she puts her hands on her lower back and leans in a deep stretch, groaning at her stiff muscles. Her eye catches on the container of books she brought with her and she moseys over to unpack them and stack them neatly on the table. When the box is empty, she glances inside to make sure she got everything and notices a small object at the bottom, glowing with a muted golden light.

Retrieving it, she realizes it's a skeleton key and examines it thoroughly, wondering how it got into her possession. She'd have to make the rounds with her clients and see if someone lost it. Placing it in her pocket, she looks around for her purse so she can leave only to remember she left it in the car. *Shit.* This means her keys are locked inside. Along with her phone. *Excellent.*

A look at her watch confirms how late it is (just after midnight), and she plops down in a chair to figure out what to do. She really doesn't want to disturb the household, but she doesn't much like the idea of spending the night in the library, either. Mrs. Kettle had brought her snacks earlier, but her rumbling stomach makes it clear it's been too long; she wants real food.

Grimacing, Iris heads to the intercom and searches for the button which will buzz in Mrs. Kettle's office. It's possible she's still up and working in there, right? But, nothing happens. Iris waits another minute before trying one more time, and when there is still no response, she curses. Spending the night in the library it is. However, she needs to find a bathroom and maybe she could find her way to the kitchen and scrounge up some food.

She twists the knob on one of the double doors leading into the house only to find it locked. *Luck be a lady, my ass, Blue Eyes. Luck is a bitch.* A vibration in her pocket reminds her of the key hidden in there, and she snags it with a finger, taking it out. The golden glow is even more pronounced now, and it's buzzing in a low hum. She feels as though the key is telling her to use it on the door. Smacking her forehead, she admonishes herself for letting her imagination get away from her.

The feeling grows stronger, and she figures, why the hell not? There is no one there to know she decided to follow the instructions of an inanimate object. Inserting the key into the lock, she rotates it until she hears a click, then tries the handle again. This time, it opens, except . . . this isn't the hallway she'd seen before. It's the only door from the library to the house, though. She blinks a couple of times and shakes her head. *I must be deliriously tired.*

The impressive gold and cream foyer is like nothing she's ever seen before and it certainly doesn't fit the timeline of this castle. There is another set of doors across from her, made of carved, gold brushed material. The details of the room draw her in to inspect them closer. She grabs the key before taking a turn about the space but, when the gets back to where she started, the library doors are no longer there. Okaaaaaay. *Am I on an episode of one of those prank shows?* With eleven sisters, and their natural instinct to rile each other up, it certainly wouldn't surprise her. The key starts up again and she figures it wants the same thing it did before. Sidling up to one of the doors, she bends to peer at the lock and sees a little carving depicting the key she holds in her hand.

She unlocks and opens the door, ready for another big surprise. Instead, she finds herself in the hallway she'd expected to find when she first stepped from the library. *Well, that was anticlimactic.* Her imagination is clearly limited, she thinks, reminding herself that's why Pippa is the novelist.

Getting back to her original goal, she wanders a few minutes until she finally discovers a powder room. After using the bathroom and washing her hands, she heads back out on her little journey. Navigating through the house is confusing, and she is starting to not only despair of ever finding the kitchen, but of not being able to return to the library. Ah ha! She finally peeks in a random doorway and sees the beautiful sight of a refrigerator. Practically skipping over to it, she opens it and grins at the shelves full of fresh fruit. *Score!*

"Who the fuck are you?" a gruff voice booms, causing Iris to scream and drop the orange in her hand when she jumps about a foot.

"Um..." She's at a loss for words as she stares up at the biggest man she's ever seen, into searing blue eyes, almost hidden by his overgrown, dark-blond hair and scraggly beard. He looks like a beast or a Yeti. Never having been a fan of scruff, Iris is floored when she's hit by a wall of lust. "Iris," she blurts out.

"The book girl?" he asks.

Iris frowns. "If you mean the art expert you hired to catalogue and appraise your library, then yes."

The Yeti's facial hair twitches. There is too much of it for her to get a read on his expression, but she can almost swear she sees amusement in his eyes until they narrow suspiciously. "Why aren't you in the library? Better yet, what are you doing in my fucking house this late?"

Annoyed by his attitude, she considers making a snide comment but decides it would take too much brain power for being after midnight and simply not worth it. So, she settles on the blatant truth. "I locked my keys and phone in my car and I didn't want to disturb anyone. I was going to stay in the library until morning when I could ask about calling someone to come take care of it. But, I'm hungry."

"You're stuck here." It's a statement, not a question.

Iris responds anyway, "No, I—"

"—You're stuck here," Yeti repeats, cutting her off. Before she can make any kind of a comeback, he closes the gap between them, lifts her by the waist as though she weighs nothing, and deposits her on a counter top. When he lets go, she's tingling from where his hands had been on her body. "Stay."

Iris gasps in outrage. "You can't just tell me to stay. I'm not a dog!"

His eyes do a slow perusal of her from head to toe, the blue of his eyes practically glowing with heat. "No, you're not. You're all woman." His gravelly voice has lost the angry edge, leaving a rough, sultry sound that she can practically feel abrading her skin. In the most delicious way.

Her stomach chooses this moment to grumble again and he points the finger of one large hand at her. "Don't move." Much to her annoyance, she doesn't. Her stupid body has evidently short-circuited her brain. She sits and watches as he moves about the kitchen; removing a pan, eggs, vegetables, and other ingredients. She rubs her tired eyes as she watches him, convinced she is seeing things that aren't there when it looks as though a plate is handed to him, rather than him reaching in and pulling it out. The stove lights on its own and she scrutinizes the walls, looking for a button like the ones that ignite a fireplace.

The Yeti sets about making her an omelet and her mouth waters. At the food. Not at the very fine ass encased in well-worn jeans. He finishes the meal and sets it on the large kitchen table, then picks her up and puts her in a chair in front of it. "I can walk, you know," she mutters. "I don't even know your name, and you're hauling me around like a rag doll."

"Archer, and it's simply easier to put you where I want you." He shrugs. Even his name is sexy? Luck needs a spectacular bitch slap.

Iris decides to ignore him and digs right into the fluffiest, most scrumptious omelet she's ever had; she moans in delight. The sound of a chair flying backward and crashing into a wall has her head whipping up in alarm. Archer is standing at the end of the table taking in deep, quick breaths, the chair he'd apparently been sitting in, now in pieces behind him.

"Stay in here," he growls before marching over to the door. He throws her one last warning glance before he disappears.

Iris leans back in her chair, bewildered by what is happening. There is still some food on her plate, however, and not willing to waste it, she goes back to eating, humming a Disney tune that suddenly popped into her head. When she finishes, Archer still hasn't returned, so she takes her dish to the sink and washes it, setting it on the counter to dry.

Finding this whole situation unsettling, she decides to disobey Mr. Sexy McGrowl and return to the library. As she leaves the kitchen, she could swear she hears a low murmur of voices conversing behind her but when she looks, it stops and she doesn't see anyone. She lectures herself about getting more sleep and not imagining things as she walks through the castle. She'd tried to pay attention when wandering before and only makes two wrong turns before she arrives at her destination. Before her hand can touch the knob, she's hauled backwards, spun around, and thrown over a shoulder, her face suddenly staring at a familiar, very tight derriere.

"What the fuck?" she screeches, for which she gets a smack on her ass.

"Watch your language, Iris," Archer warns. "It's not befitting of a queen."

"Since I wouldn't wish to lose any of my sisters, I assure— oomph—will you stop bouncing me around so much?" she snaps. Pacified when he slows his steps, she starts to thank him until he chooses to hold her steady with his big palm on her butt. Flustered, she runs through what she was attempting to talk about. Right. "As I was saying, I'm not likely to be queen."

Archer mumbles something almost unintelligible, but it sounds like it might have been, "We'll just see about that."

He comes to a set of stairs and swings her down to be cradled in his arms while he jogs up to the next floor. She should probably be focusing on what the hell is happening, but at the moment, she can't do anything but stare, open-mouthed, speechless at the beauty of the face attached to the strong body she is nestled against. Archer had shaved and is now only sporting a slight darkening of scruff, and his hair is pulled back into man-bun-type-thing. Every chiseled feature is on display; his angular jaw, full lips, patrician nose, and those unbelievably blue eyes surrounded by dark lashes, despite his blond hair. A long, corded neck leads to strong shoulders, and reeeeeally nice biceps. He's, to put it bluntly, fucking gorgeous.

He enters a room and the next thing she knows; Iris finds herself dropped onto the mattress of a massive bed. She glances around quickly, and it clicks that she is most likely in his bedroom. He's standing over her, hands on his hips, studying her with clear indecision. Behind him, her eye is drawn to a large painting of a rose. Her mind starts to play tricks on her again because . . . *is that rose wilting*?! She begins to crawl backwards on the bed, intending to climb off on the other side, but Archer snatches her ankle and keeps her from going anywhere.

"You're mine, beauty." The words have a ring of finality to them, as though there is no question; it simply is.

"I don't think so," she replies crisply. Staring up at him, she knows she should be freaking out, screaming bloody murder or something but . . . ugh, why does he have to be so magnetically attractive? She feels a pull to him she's never felt with another person before. Archer leans over her, his eyes probing, searching for something.

"I don't have the fucking time to court or woo you, Iris," he says abruptly. "Besides, it will have the same result. There is no fucking way I'm letting you go."

"You can't just . . . keep me here," she declares. To her mortification, her voice is more puzzled than seething. She can't possibly be considering—this is crazy—there's no way. A persistent little voice in her head would like to know why. She does a mental head shake. The voice must be connected to her hormones because he is lighting up every fucking nerve ending like fireworks.

He opens his mouth and by the obstinate gleam in his eye,

she's pretty sure he is going to flatly disagree. Then his mouth closes and his face turns cunning. "I'll tell you what, beauty," he drawls, "if you can resist me, I'll leave you alone and let you walk right out the door in the morning."

If it were anyone else, this would be a no-brainer, but Iris is well aware of the pitfalls in making this deal, namely the fact that he isn't even touching her and she's practically panting like a bitch in heat. Finally, she decides to let her inhibitions go and just give in. Let's not pretend that his whole alpha "You're mine" attitude isn't sexy as fuck.

She grasps his shirt with both hands and tugs sharply, throwing him off balance so his big body falls onto her. "You win," she purrs. His eyes light up as though he's won the lottery. Although, judging by his castle and his amazing library of priceless books, he doesn't need it. But, you get the point. He smiles and any sign of the Yeti disappears, except in his eyes. They are the same piercing blue, gazing deep into her soul.

Lifting himself onto his elbows, he runs a finger down her cheek, her neck, collar bone, and over her breast, tweaking the nipple and making her catch her breath. "You are so fucking beautiful. My beauty," he groans before his mouth crashes down on hers.

His kisses are drugging and consume every part of her, making her forget everything except him. He tastes like peppermint and something she instinctively knows is just *him*. He takes his time, taking her clothes off piece by piece, kissing, licking, and biting each uncovered spot with a growl. By the time she's naked and he sits back with a satisfied expression, she's a quivering mass of want.

Stripping, he joins her on the bed, scooting down and shouldering her legs open to wedge between them. His hot breath bathes her pussy and she moans, her hips lifting involuntarily. Archer turns his head and licks the delicate skin of her inner thigh, then bites gently, leaving a mark of possession. Without warning, he puts his mouth on her, his mouth wide, taking as much of her pussy as he can and sucking. Iris cries out and bucks up, whimpering when Archer uses his hands on her hips to keep her anchored to the bed. His tongue laps at her, long, slow licks from top to bottom, interspersed with plunges of his stiffened tongue inside her. He drives her up and when she's sitting high atop the pinnacle, he licks torturously around her clit without touching it. "You have the prettiest pussy, beauty. So wet, pink, and plump." His voice is dark and deep, saturated with need. "Do you want to come?"

Iris shouts a garbled agreement, her head thrashing on the pillow. "Whose name are you going to be screaming when you come, beauty?"

"Yo—yours," she pants.

"Damn fucking straight." He wraps his lips around her little bundle of nerves and sucks it hard. She screams his name as her body splinters apart, like a firecracker, each little electrified piece of her raining from the peak.

Archer climbs her body and revels in the sight of his woman as she feels such ultimate pleasure, all because of him. It's a primitive, primal thing, the need to be everything to your mate, as much as the need to breed. He grabs Iris's chin and holds her head so they are visually connected. "I'm fucking you bare, beauty. You're going to give me a son. I need an heir."

"An heir?"

"I have to take a wife in the next few days or I won't be allowed to ascend to the throne. I'd resigned myself to it, then you came along, and I knew you were going to be mine. You deserve everything I have, Iris. You deserve to be my queen."

"I don't need anything, but . . . you." She looks shocked at the revelation. "I need you?"

Archer winks. "I'm going to spend the rest of my life making sure that is always true."

~

Archer puts two plates with omelets on a tray with bowls of fruit, muffins, and a couple glasses of orange juice. He sternly tells himself to calm the fuck down and stop acting like a teenager. Except, he feels like one, unable to control his physical response to even the thought of Iris St. Claire.

The first time he spoke to her, there was something in her voice that called to him, he'd been so flustered, his voice had been gruff as he struggled for words, so his responses were clipped one word answers. He knew he'd come across like a real bastard, and he'd had every intention of rectifying it during their next conversation. He'd gotten off of the phone and researched her, learning as much as he could, before calling up a friend and having him run an in-depth check on her. He didn't care what people would say about it; he was determined to know as much about her as possible so he'd have the best advantage when convincing her she was his.

Unfortunately, they'd only had one more phone call, and it hadn't gone much better because she'd been asking to push the job off a few weeks. Apparently, she'd found a stash of antique books and first editions in a hidden spot of the castle she'd been working in at the time. Archer was already impatient to have her, the delay irritated the fuck out of him. He tried to agree graciously, but once again, he was sure he'd given her the impression he was a beast.

Last night, he'd dreamed of them together. It had been incredible and he was sure the real thing would be a million times more so. This morning he'd seen her car parked out front and was surprised she would be here so early, but when he popped into the library, he'd found her slumped over a table, fast asleep with her head pillowed in her arms. He knew she was passionate about her job and he was willing to bet she'd fallen asleep while working late and had been there all night.

He decides to wake her with breakfast. This is his chance to undo some of the damage he's done. After cooking, he makes his way to the library, carefully balancing the tray. At the library, he pushes on the door he left partially open and backs his way in. She is sitting up, but she looks dazed as though she is just waking. The dishes clink and she whips around at the sound, her light green eyes much more alert. They widen as they drink in the sight of him and he is immensely grateful for the tray hiding the evidence of his desire for her.

He smiles and takes the tray to her table, setting it down gently. She looks at it and then back up at Archer with raised brows. "Omelets?" she asks with a little dreaminess in her tone.

He nods and goes to her, squatting in front of her. "It's nice to finally meet you in person, Iris." He lifts her hand to his lips and brushes a soft kiss across the tender skin. When he looks up again, her face is soft and almost shy as she returns his smile. "I want to apologize for acting like such a jackass the two times we spoke. My only excuse is that you tie me in knots and I—" He stops, unsure how forward he should be. *Oh, fuck it.* "I've wanted you from the moment I first heard your voice, Iris. I knew, in that moment, I knew you were meant to be mine."

A blinding smile breaks across her face and she throws her arms around Archer, nearly knocking him to the ground. "You're right, Archer. I'm all yours, as much as you're mine." She leans back and looks at him warily. "Right?"

Archer uses a hand on the back of her neck to pull her

forward and seal their mouths together. Against her lips, he mumbles, "Completely yours, beauty."

Eventually, they break apart in need of oxygen. Archer runs a finger from her cheek down to her breast, over her nipple, circling it, before going back up. He cups her face between his large palms, gazing deeply into her eyes. "I have to return home in two months," he tells her. "My father wants to step down, and we'll have the coronation shortly after."

Iris looks adorably confused when she clarifies, "Wait, you're a prince?"

Archer shrugs sheepishly. "You know how it is. I'd rather meet people without their preconceived notions of royalty, or worse, be on the receiving end of their ploys to use me."

Not able to argue with his logic, Iris nods.

"I want you to come with me, beauty." He watches for signs she might be freaking out, when he sees none, he forges ahead. "As my wife, Iris. I want you to be my queen, to give me an heir and a spare, and couple little girls to spoil, who look just like their mother." He grins.

"You want four?" Iris asks thoughtfully.

"At least," he admits.

Iris grins and pecks him on the lips. "We'd better get started on those right away then."

Archer laughs and reaches for her but she bats his arms away and pulls over the tray of food. "First, you feed me."

He leans in, his lips close to her ear, and runs his tongue along the shell. "I'll fill you with food, beauty. Then I'm going to take you to bed and fill you with something else," he informs her. Iris starts choking on her bite of muffin, her cheeks turning bright red, causing Archer to laugh boisterously.

He fulfilled both promises.

1 . . . 2 . . . 3 . . . swoon

PIPPA

Apparently, Jenna and Iris have found the loves of their lives. I would have thought my parents would balk at so many cases of "insta-love" among their daughters. Then, I remember, A, they met and married in less than two months and B, they are hopeless romantics. I sigh and slide down into a comfy, overstuffed chair by my window, grabbing one of my new books. I crack it open, but my mind wanders to the events of the evening.

Oliver gave me first editions of four of my favorite books. As if it wasn't a sweet enough gesture, then he told me the men in the stories were incredibly lucky to win the hearts of these women. When a man finds a smart, courageous, independent, unbelievably gorgeous woman, trying to change her, or letting her go, was the stupidest fucking things they could ever do.

Then he kissed me senseless and left.

What did I do next? *See chapter title above*.

Damn that man for being so irresistible.

I have eleven sisters . . . six down . . . five more.

But, who is counting?

Who is counting? Me.

OLIVER

The look on Pippa's face when I left last night was absolutely priceless. I figured it was better to quit while I was ahead, so I kissed the fuck out of her and left her still in a daze.

An arrogant grin has been permanently painted on my face today. I can't wait to see her look like that when I'm buried deep inside her. I blow out a breath and run my hands through my hair, irritated at not being able to concentrate on getting any work done, and now I'm sporting a fucking hard on. I need to get it together, or next thing I know, I'll be daydreaming and drawing hearts around Pippa's name.

I'm saved from my thoughts of losing my man card when Simon walks in and flops down on my couch. I raise a single eyebrow at him. "Something on your mind?" I ask, welcoming the distraction.

Simon's expression turns dark and he practically snarls when he looks back at the door to my office. Following his line of sight, I just barely catch Abbi scurrying away. *When did this happen?* "No," he growls in answer to my question. "I simply think people shouldn't stay out all night with who the fuck knows who, and then come to work dragging and tired."

Hmm . . . I wonder if Wilhelm is paying attention. A jolt stings me in my chest, right behind my pocket, and I almost berate Wilhelm for being a little bastard and shocking me. I catch myself in time and avoid indulging Simon's theory that I'm losing my mind.

"Wilder called. He's on his way here." Simon changes the subject. "He's bringing new contracts."

"For the new expansions, I presume?" Wilder is an architect and owns an incredibly successful construction company. He's going to head up the expansion projects on several of my company's buildings.

"Yeah."

I nod. "You told him to get with Piper for the interior design?" I confirm.

Simon waves me off. "I told him months ago. He's already been working with her for a few weeks now."

At Simon's words, Wilhelm practically does a little dance in my pocket. *All right, all right, calm the fuck down.* Right, Piper is the next sister on the agenda, I suddenly remember. But the little shit just gets even crazier when Wilder strolls through the door a minute later. He's dressed in jeans, boots, and a leather jacket, having just come from a job site. I scrutinize him for a second because something looks different. Same brown hair, medium height, brown eyes, and toned muscles from working construction and his MMA training.

"Hey," he says, striding over and shaking my hand.

"Wilder," I greet as I take the folders he proffers me. "Take a seat and I'll sign these now." Another glance and I realize what it is, he looks a little gaunt and from the weariness in his eyes, it's clear he is exhausted. "You okay, man?" I enquire.

He scrubs his hands up and down his face and nods. "I haven't been sleeping well, but the problem should be resolved tonight."

"Woman trouble?" I guess and give him an empathetic smile.

He laughs. "Not to your caliber, dude. You any closer to putting a ring on your woman's finger?"

"Any day now," I smirk.

This gets Simon's attention as well, and he eagerly asks, "Really? Was it—"

"—Don't you have work to do?" I cut him off. He shrugs and stays planted on the couch, but keeps his mouth shut.

I open the first folder and take the papers out of the pocket. Wilhelm shocks me again. *Ouch. Knock it off, jackass.* I sign the papers and am returning them to the folder when it hits me. Wilhelm seems to want to go with Wilder instead of Piper. *That's new.* I mentally shrug and while Wilder and Simon talk, I drop the key into the folder.

I convince Pippa to go to dinner with me and we go to a romantic little restaurant. While we are there, we witness an elaborate set up for a man to ask his girlfriend to marry him. It makes me realize, a romantic proposal could only help my chances.

When I drop her off, I leave her with a scorching kiss before driving home making plans for when my twelve days are up.

After tonight, there will only be four.

But, who is counting?

Oh, yes....*me*.

Meanwhile...

Wilder walks into his office and tosses the folders onto his desk. Something small flies out of the bottom one, hitting the wall behind his desk and falling to the floor. He walks around the furniture and bends at the knees to pick it up. It's a key, a skeleton key. It's like nothing he's ever seen before and he scrutinizes it as he stands back up and sits in his chair. Where did it come from? He'd taken the contracts to Oliver, then he'd left them in the car while he checked out three different active construction sites.

He was supposed to meet with Piper, Oliver's recommended interior designer for his projects. Normally, he doesn't let the client dictate who he works with but, he trusts Oliver implicitly. Of course, he did his due diligence anyway, and Piper's portfolio is extremely impressive for being so young. It had only taken one minute in her presence to know she was his. And after spending more time with her, he became even more captivated. She was sweet, smart, and she made him laugh. And, she was insanely hot. Let's not beat around the bush, he was completely and irrevocably in love with her. But, circumstances had kept him from pursuing her. Until now.

The corners of his mouth turn down in a frown as he thinks about her. She's also been very dependable, so it worried him when she'd missed their appointment. Do to trouble with one of his projects, he called and texted her, asking to push the time of their meeting. He'd never heard back. Picking up his cell phone, he calls her for the fourth time and still no answer, prompting him to leave a fourth message. He shoots off a text to her, as well. He doesn't wanted to worry her family if it is nothing but, if she doesn't get in touch with him soon, he'll have to check and see if she's contacted them.

As he stares at his phone, it pings with an email. Tension seeps out of his shoulders when he sees the final payment from a client who'd been the biggest pain in the ass. Not only did she change her mind at every turn, but she blatantly came on to him every time he was forced to see her, despite him turning her down repeatedly. She'd started asking his opinion on every decision she was given, which wouldn't necessarily be unusual, but for the fact that it was literally *every* time. She'd make offhand remarks about it being important that he liked the house, too.

She'd made him so uncomfortable, it was why he held off asking Piper out. He didn't want her on the crazy lady's radar. Finally, unable to wait until the job was done, he'd handed her off to his partner, Phoenix, for which he still hadn't been forgiven. Phoenix told him he was being a coward, that Piper wouldn't appreciate the fact that he hadn't slain his own dragon. He'd snorted, ignoring the first part, but agreeing she was definitely a fire-breathing dragon.

The job is done now, and he doesn't have to deal with her anymore. Wilder stands, the key still in hand, and absentmindedly slips it into his pocket.

His business is in a sprawling ranch house not far from town. When he renovated it, he added a parking lot to the back and there is a door that opens directly into his personal office. Since he came in through it, he doesn't know if the rest of the floor is cleared out of employees. He doesn't want to lock up without checking, so he walks to the door that leads to the hallway behind his office, grasps the handle and tugs. When it doesn't open as expected, gravity throws him forward and he almost goes head first into the door. Trying the knob again, he isn't able to turn it and even though it supposed to lock from the inside, he isn't able to find the mechanism. *What the hell?* He scratches his head and looks around as though he'll find the answer somewhere else in the room. His eyes eventually fall to the clock on his desk. It's just after midnight. He's been up since five in the morning, so he chalks it up to being overtired. Facing the door again, he gives the handle one last twist and tugs. Nothing. Frustrated, he rests a palm on the door and almost falls on his face when it pushes open. He starts to wonder if the universe is intent on getting its kicks from seeing him break his neck.

Catching his balance, his jaw drops when he gets a look at the luxurious foyer he suddenly finds himself in. The gold and creams scheme is detailed and only just barely on the classy side versus gaudy. A massive, crystal chandelier hangs above him, and he quickly steps to the side so he isn't in its immediate drop radius. *Simply hedging my bets.*

The slam of a door startles him, particularly when said door is no longer there. He groans in frustration, convinced his mind is playing tricks on him. With a tall set of gold, double doors being the only exit now, he attempts to open them and finds them locked. *Shocker.* A hum breaks the silence and Wilder's ears perk, listening. It's the sound of something vibrating and it's coming from his pocket. The key. Could it be? It would be awfully coincidental. He shakes his head at himself. It would be par for the course of weirdness; he might as well give it a shot. Extracting the key from his pocket, he dips down to examine the lock and seeing the matching carving, he inserts it into the hole. The tumblers click and he's able to open the door.

Hesitantly going forward, he finds himself in a bedroom—one he doesn't recognize. The figure lying on the bed, however, he definitely recognizes her. Padding across the thick carpet, he approaches the bed. Piper is on her back, on top of the covers, her lush, dark brown hair pulled over both shoulders, spilling down her chest. She's wearing a lavender gown, ruched and snug around her chest; the straightened, silky skirt flows down from her waist to her feet. He smiles when he sees she isn't wearing shoes; her adorable, purple-tipped toes are peeking out. His hardening cock is a familiar reaction, since everything about this woman turns him on, giving him an erection every time he sees her, hears her, even just fucking thinking about her gets him going.

She appears to be deeply asleep—her long, black lashes resting on her pale, plump cheeks, and her lips, soft in sleep, are pink and completely kissable. His eyebrows raise at the unexpected sight of a rose clutched between her hands as they rest, crossed beneath her breasts. Something about the whole scene . . . the way she's dressed, her position, even the blue, silk panels hanging from the canopy, the weaved rod iron headboard which looks like a thicket of roses and thorns. It all reminds him of something, but he isn't able to get a grasp on it.

He sits down next to her and stares, awed by her beauty as always, enjoying the site of her so peaceful in sleep. But, he wants to see her sparkling green eyes, so he runs a finger over her forehead, down her cheek, and across her delectable lips. No response.

"Piper," he calls softly. "Baby?" This time, he leans over

and brushes his lips across her forehead, but she doesn't stir. *She must really be in a deep sleep.* Maybe . . . he has an idea, though it seems ludicrous. He stares at her mouth for a moment, then decides to try it. His head dips again, intent on giving her a kiss. Before their mouths can connect, a blast of hot wind blows him right off the bed.

"Son of a bitch!" he curses as he lands hard on the ground. *Are you happy now, universe?*

"The universe is the least of your worries, Wilder."

His head whips up and he's staring into the violet eyes of... "Maggie?" he croaks.

A woman stands at another entrance to the room, a set of doors leading to a balcony. He almost doesn't recognize his obnoxious client in the dragon skin body suit she's somehow poured herself into. Let's just clarify, no one...*no one*, should ever wear this outfit, doesn't matter how fit you are, it will still be ugly as sin. This goes triple for Maggie. He's not being insensitive or judgmental. It's simply a fact. Maggie's body had taken a hit from the years of hard drinking, bad food, and no exercise. Somehow, she manages to look emaciated everywhere except the spots where she has sagging pockets of fat. *See? Fact. You feel me?*

"You didn't think I would learn about your precious Piper, Wilder?" she sneers. Anger courses through him as he gets to his feet and takes a menacing step in her direction.

"What the fuck are you doing here, Maggie?" he spits.

She glances at his beautiful, sleeping Piper and when she looks back at him, her eyes are practically spitting fire. "You're coming with me," she says in a low tone, sending a cold shiver down his spine. "You can't kiss her."

"Maggie, you've lost your fucking mind," Wilder bellows as he stalks towards her. "I'm not going anywhere with you."

An evil grin slashes across her face. "Now, you deal with me, oh Wilder. And, all the powers of hell." She backs up, out to the balcony and sits on the railing, still smiling malevolently. Without warning, she falls backward into the dark night.

"No!" Wilder yells as he dashes outside. He knows it's too late to save her, but the white knight inside him has to try. Rushing up to the balcony, he grips the rail and looks over, only to be, once again, knocked to the ground by a rush of heated wind.

A large shadow looms over him and he looks up at the source. He blinks, shakes his head to clear what must be a hallucination, and blinks again.

Nope. Still staring at a fucking dragon. A flying dragon.

He jumps to his feet and glances around wildly, trying to figure out how to make himself wake up from this dream. His eyes land on a sword, propped against the wall in the corner of the balcony. His eyes narrow on the weapon and he swiftly walks over and picks it up. Words are carved in the gleaming silver, Sword of Truth. The feeling of familiarity begins to nag him again, but with more force this time.

Maggie, the malevolent dragon, as he's christened her, hovers over the side of the balcony, watching him. He lifts the sword and she breathes fire, just missing him by inches, and it singes the hair on his arm.

"Are you going to slay the dragon?" she hisses.

Wilder considers his options, reading the words on the sword again. An idea pops into his head. "I don't think so," he says thoughtfully. "In fact, I don't even think this is my fantasy. You are a product of our mixed imaginations. I don't need to take you out, I have no desire to kill anyone"—he looks her over with disgust—"or any *thing*. I'm just going to be honest." He drops the saber on the ground and turns back to the room. "Go back to your cave, Puff."

She shrieks in outrage but he tunes her out and focuses on the gorgeous sleeping woman. He returns to his previous spot on the bed and picks up where he left off, dropping his head and covering her mouth with his own.

Piper gasps and tries to sit up suddenly, effectively banging their heads together. "Ouch." She winces, putting her hand to her head. Wilder scoots back and lets her sit up fully as he swallows a chuckle, then grasps her face between his palms.

He kisses the abused spot, then looks into the depths of her green pools. "Are you all right?" he queries before indulging himself in another kiss to her sweet mouth.

"Um hmm," she mumbles against his lips, then pulls back. "Wilder? What's going on?"

"Well," he drawls, "I considered slaying a dragon for you. Then, I decided I had a far greater weapon with which to win the fair princess."

She giggles as he stands and does an exaggerated bow. "I'll bite," she says, then giggles again at his raised brow and very interested expression. "What is this magic weapon you think is going to win me over?"

Wilder slowly gets down on one knee by the side of the bed, winking at her as her eyes grow big and round. He takes her hands and kisses each one in the center of the palm.

"I'll tell you the honest truth, baby. I've loved you since the moment I met you, Piper. I wanted to make sure there weren't any forests of thorns in our way before I took you and made you mine."

Her jaw had been slowly dropping but now, it snaps shut and she glares at him. "Make me yours? Do I get a say?"

He shrugs. "Not really."

She sputters but doesn't seem to have a response, so he decides to move on and gets on on the bed, his body covering hers, forcing her to lay back again. He holds some of his weight off of her, but makes sure he's pressing into her, connecting them from head to toe. When his hard on settles in the cleft of her thighs, she gasps and shudders.

"You can't deny it, baby. Admit it," he whispers. "You feel it in your heart, and I'm betting your pussy is drenched right now, because your body knows it, too. You're mine." He starts to kiss his way down her body, his hands traveling all over her, wanting to feel every inch of her. When he reaches the end of the ruching on her top and the skirt begins to flow, he frowns at the diaphones material. He clutches a handful of the lavender silk and rips it from the seam, tearing the whole skirt down the center. Wilder grins at the surprise underneath.

"Hey!" Piper exclaims, her head lifting and directing a pout in his direction. But, she seems to lose all thought when his hot mouth lands on her naked pussy. He groans at the proof he was right; she's completely soaked. She tastes like peaches and cream, and he can't get enough. He's been dreaming about this every damn night. Unable to sleep without fantasizing about fucking her until she's screaming his name. Deciding not to waste time, he attacks her pussy, rapidly driving her up and pushing her over the ledge.

The sound of his name falling from her lips in ecstasy almost drives him to orgasm, but he manages to hang on to a thread of control. Crawling up, he finds a side zipper on the top of the dress. He lowers it, then impatiently rips in apart to get to her breasts. They are even more gorgeous than he'd imagined; full and round, with tight, pink nipples, the same shade as her lips. Drawing one into his mouth, he moans, discovering they taste every bit as delicious.

He switches nipples and sucks it deep before letting it go with a pop. "Baby," he growls. She's too lost in sensation to hear him, so he pinches a nipple hard and speaks louder this time. "Piper!"

She shudders, as much from the stinging pain as sparks of pleasure elicited from his actions. "What?" she pants, trying to focus on him and not the bulge of his cock cradled in the V of her thighs.

"I'm not going to take you until you agree to marry me," he states nonchalantly. As though he hadn't just turned her world upside down.

"You're asking me to marry you?" she asks incredulously.

"Yup," he answers in the same cavalier tone.

"I—yes."

Astonished, he asks, "Just like that?"

She nods. "You were honest, so I'm going to be, too. I want to marry you. I want to be yours. Done. End of story." Her green eyes become mischievous. "Now, are you going to take me or are you all talk and no action?" she taunts.

Action, she thinks later as she lays replete with pleasure and utterly exhausted. Definitely action.

A tingling sensation in her lips wakes Piper, and she rubs her eyes sleepily, shifting to try and relieve some of the pressure in her body. *Stupid, fucking erotic fantasies.*

"Baby?" A low masculine voice washes over her and every nerve in her body sings. "Piper?"

She opens her bleary eyes and finds herself staring at the most amazing brown eyes. Ones she had countless dreams about, ones she'd fallen hopelessly in love with. "Wilder?"

He beams at her. "Hey, sleeping beauty." Then, he frowns. "You feel asleep in the waiting room of my office. Were you here all evening, baby?"

She thinks for a minute, trying to clear the fog of sleep from her mind. "Um, yeah. I had a cancellation and was already here when I got your text, so I decided to wait for you."

His frown deepens and he growls, "Why didn't you respond, Piper? I've been going out of my mind with worry."

Confusion clouds her face. She did respond. She's sure she

had. Picking up her phone, she swipes the screen to turn it on, but nothing happens. "Shit," she murmurs before looking up and smiling at him sheepishly. "I sent the text and then my phone died. It must have still been in the process of sending. I'm so sorry I worried you, Wilder."

His face softens but his eyes are completely serious. "I don't want you to let your phone die while you're out by yourself, baby. I can't stomach even the possibility of something happening to you. I'm not all that happy you were alone in my office so late. Anyone could have walked in."

Piper's heart starts to beat a little faster the more he says, he sounds like he . . . like he might care about her. As more than a colleague. She tells herself not to hope but it's impossible when she's already owned by him, even if he doesn't know it.

"Your secretary locked up before she left. We both thought you'd be here sooner."

He caresses her face, and his eyes follow his fingers as they run through her dark hair, pulling it forward over her shoulders. They linger on her breasts for half a beat, then they jump to her lips and seem glued there. She's taken off guard when he lunges forward and kisses her deeply. Her head spins and she grabs onto his biceps to steady herself. He finally releases her mouth when they need to come up for oxygen. "I'm sorry you had to wait for me, baby. But, fuck, I'm so glad you're here."

"You are?" *Please, please, please,* she chants in her head. *Please say what I hope you're going to say.*

"This may be a little overwhelming but, I need you to listen with your heart and not your head, okay?" he petitions her earnestly. Too busy chanting to speak, she nods.

"I'm so in love with you, Piper. You consume my every thought, every dream. All I can think about is making love to you, marrying you, and starting a family with you. You're mine already, even if you haven't realized it. So, listen to your heart, baby, because I know, without a shadow of a doubt, it beats for me, just like mine does for you."

"Wow," she breathes. "You kiss a girl awake and then make a speech like that. How could she possibly turn you down? Of course, it certainly doesn't hurt that you're hot." She grins even as she blushes from being so bold.

Wilder laughs and his lips quirk up into a crooked smile. "Baby, you're one to talk. You're a walking wet dream, and I have the feeling I'm going to be in a constant state of arousal for the rest of our lives."

"I guess, I'll have to spend the rest of my life with you so I can take care of this little problem then," she says cheekily. Wilder throws his head back and laughs a full out belly laugh.

"I love you so fucking much." He stands and holds out a hand to her. "Let me take you home, baby. *Our* home." Piper takes his hand and steps into a life where fantasy has met reality.

Principles for orgasms seems like a fair trade

~~~~

OLIVER

"Fucking gorgeous," I growl, burying my face in Pippa's masses of long, chocolate brown hair and inhaling her sweet jasmine scent. "Five nights, baby." An evening breeze blows through the open doors to my terrace, cooling my heated skin.

"Wh—what?" She stumbles over her words, her breathing choppy, her sable eyes are glazed over with satisfaction. I may not be willing to fuck her until we are married, but it doesn't mean I can't make her come. As often and as hard as possible. There are few sights I crave more than seeing Pippa come... though none come to mind at the moment. Lifting my head, I remove my hand from her slick pussy and raise it to my mouth.

I groan as her taste explodes on my tongue. I'd taken Pippa to dinner, then brought her back to our house to spend some uninterrupted time alone. I don't know what I was thinking. I need to take her home. *Now.*

"Five nights, then you're mine," I answer her. There are still four sisters to work through, then I'll be dragging her—kicking and screaming if need be—to a priest and tying her to

153

me permanently. Then I'm going to take her to our home and make her scream in an entirely and much more enjoyable way.

"You sure are cocky, Oliver," she mutters as she squirms in my lap, though, I notice she doesn't try to get up.

"Confident, baby," I say with a grin. I kiss her lips quick and hard, then help her stand, laughing when she looks as though she trying to decide whether to pout or be angry. Getting to my feet, I can't resist pulling her back into my arms. "Why are you still fighting me, Pippa?" I'm determined to win her little game, but I'm curious why she's still adamantly refusing to admit she wants me as much as I want her.

She mumbles something as she tries to break my hold, but I tense my muscles, keeping her caged in. "What was that, baby?" I can't help grinning when she glowers at me.

"It's the principle of the thing!" she snaps. I start laughing so hard I have to let her go so I can bend over, hands on my knees, trying to get in some air.

"You're so fucking adorable," I say when I can breathe again. "I appreciate your moral code, baby. But, in a few days, you'll be trading those principles for orgasms." I kiss her hard and fast on the mouth, then smirk. "You're getting the better end of the deal. Wouldn't you say?"

Spinning on her heel, she marches from the room, and it doesn't escape my notice that she didn't dispute my comments. I catch up to her by the door, still snickering, and place my hand on her lower back, leading her to the car.

It doesn't take long to get to the palace and when we walk into the kitchen through a back door—once a servant's entrance—we run into Pippa's other twin sisters, Odette and Shelby. They are identical in every way except Shelby wears glasses and her eyes are more sea green as opposed to Odette's darker grey-green ones. Even their hair is cut similarly, hanging straight to swish just above their shoulders. They are sitting at a table, deep in discussion and eating ice cream from the container. Pippa immediately grabs a spoon and plops down next to Shelby. She dips her spoon in for a big scoop of the chocolate and peanut butter dessert, even as she scrutinizes Odette.

"Man troubles?" she prods before sticking the utensil full of ice cream in her mouth.

Odette's head drops to bang lightly against the table. "More like wicked step-mother troubles," she groans. "Except it's worse because it's Dylan's actual mother." She sits back up and eats another bite of ice cream, her expression dark and angry.

"Is killing your mother-in-law considered matricide?" Pippa wonders aloud. I press my lips together to avoid laughing at my sweet Pippa. I'm standing off to the side, trying to remain inconspicuous as I listen.

I'm a little confused, though; I hadn't realized Odette was engaged. Are we going to be able to skip her? Wilhelm chooses that moment to be obnoxious as usual, vibrating like crazy in my pocket. *Okay, maybe not.*

"I'm not likely to find out, am I?" Odette laments. "She keeps trying to set him up with princess after princess. He refuses every time, but I'm worried she's going to convince him one of these days."

Ah, so Dylan needs a push. Wilhelm hums in agreement, and I start to watch for an opportunity to give her the key.

"I don't understand," Pippa interjects. "It's not like you aren't a 'real' princess. What's her problem?"

Odette shrugs. "Who the hell knows? I obviously don't meet her standards."

Shelby rubs a hand soothingly over her back. "Maybe there is some way to convince her you are what she wants for Dylan."

Returning her head to the table, Odette groans. "Like what? Cut myself and show her my blue blood? She'll let me bleed out while she chooses a wedding dress for the bride she handpicked."

Shelby sighs as she stands, beginning to clean up their mess, but she stops when she suddenly notices me. "Hey Oliver," she greets me with a smile.

"Shelby," I return warmly. "It's nice to see you. Are you home for a while?" Shelby is an underwater archeologist. She'd skipped several grades as a child and graduated with a Masters in Maritime Archaeology at only twenty years old. The last year and a half, she'd been on an exploratory expedition— basically modern day treasure hunting.

"Yeah, I'm spending a few weeks working with museums here and in the surrounding countries, getting the items we salvaged into the right exhibits," she explains. I vaguely wonder how that will work when it comes time for her fantasy. However, since it's clearly Odette's turn, it isn't worth pondering at the moment. I mentally shrug; Wilhelm's running this reality version of *Love Connection* anyway.

"Well, I'm sure your sisters are excited to have you home as long as they can." I stroll over to Pippa and lean down to give her a lingering kiss on the lips. When I pull back, her cheeks are flaming red and her sisters are smiling broadly at us. "I'll see you tomorrow, baby. I'm going to come by around noon and take you to lunch," I inform her. Pippa nods, still a little hazy from my kiss, it seems. It is such a huge turn on that I can affect her like this.

Looking around, I don't see a bag near Odette and her dress has no pockets. I'm stumped for a moment, then wonder if I should just give it to her. Wilhelm seems to approve of this plan, so I take the long way around the table to kiss the cheeks of each sister. I press the key into Odette's hand. "Keep this hidden. It belongs to you tonight. Trust me," I whisper. She gives me a peculiar look and I simply nod at her before taking my leave.

I go home and fall onto the couch, lying on my back and staring at the ceiling. *Five fucking nights.*

Meanwhile...

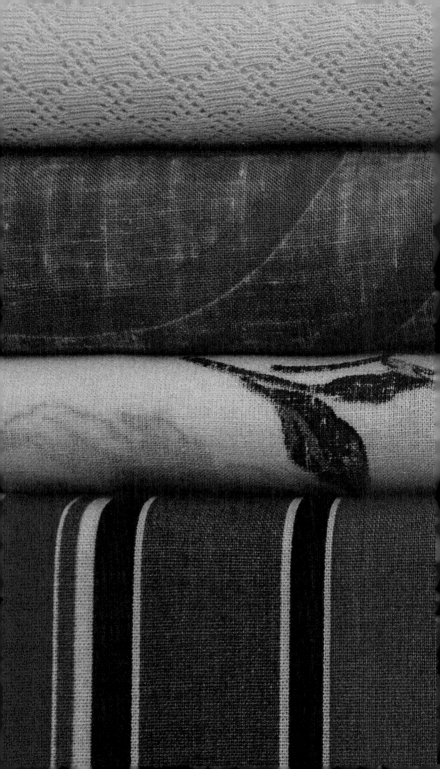

Odette's Fantasy

SPAWNED BY THE MILKMAN

Odette says goodnight to her sisters and leaves for her apartment near her old college campus. The whole way, she keeps the odd key from Oliver clutched in her fist. She didn't know what to make of it, but for some unknown reason, when he'd put the key in her hand, she felt as though it belonged there. What was it he said? It belonged to her tonight? It was a unique key, like nothing she'd ever seen before, made of gold and a heart on the top made out of an intricate designs of vines. Well, perhaps it would take her mind off of her troubles.

She'd met Dylan in college when she was a freshman, and he was a junior. They'd been dating since then, and she knew beyond a shadow of a doubt he was the only man for her. He'd never directly asked her to marry him, but he'd constantly talked about "their" future together. As though there wasn't another option but to spend it together.

She first met the old queen at his graduation, it was the first time Odette had been faced with this an attitude like this woman's. Odette felt like a bug under her shoe, although, the queen managed to do it a very passive aggressive way. Dylan hadn't been completely oblivious to it; but his mother was cunning and she knew how to subtly get her digs in, so that he didn't notice most of the time.

Odette and Dylan had planned to spend the summer together in his country, at a small cottage by the sea since he wasn't expected to ascend to the throne for a few years. The queen had been pissed, but Dylan firmly informed her they were going ahead with their plans. She'd been an occasional annoyance over the few months Odette spent there, but for the most part, it was pretty idyllic, and it was difficult to return home at the end of it.

They'd decided on a long distance relationship while Odette finished up school. She'd busted her ass to get done with her double degree in International Relations and Business a year early. After she'd graduated, she'd expected to move right away. But, Dylan had been cagey about it and encouraged her to take her time. When they were together, he was every bit her Dylan, but she fretted every time he or she left from a visit to each other. She'd gone to him less and less frequently, not willing to put up with his mother for fear she'd be thrown in a dungeon for assaulting the queen.

Pulling into her parking lot, she is forced to drive to the very back to the only open spaces. After shutting the car off, Odette sighs and looks down at the key. What this object could do to help her was a mystery and more than likely, the answer was nothing. She tosses the key into her purse, gets out of the car and freezes in complete shock when the skies open up and start pouring down rain. By the time the use of her faculties returns and she sprints to her building and up the stairs to her door, she is soaked through. Her reflection in the window next to her door confirms she looks exactly as she feels —like a drowned rat.

"Aaaaargh!" she screams. This is a fitting end to her shitty day. Rooting through her purse, she finds her house keys and tries to unlock her door. It doesn't work. *Really? Going to kick me when I'm down?* Pushing her wet hair out of her face, she drops her purse to the ground in front of her and bends down to look directly at the lock as she tries the key again. Same result. She's standing on a little, covered walkway, but the rain is fierce and the angle is still pelting her with sheets of water. Lightning illuminates the area all around her and thunder booms, causing her to jump. Her nerves are a jumble so she doesn't notice the vibrating and glowing object in her purse.

Tears start to course down her cheeks and she leans her forehead on the door, staring at the ground. It's then that she notices the glow coming from her purse and squats down to investigate. The skeleton key is sitting atop everything else in her bag, putting off a dim golden light and, when she picks it up, she realizes it's subtly humming with energy. Out of nowhere, the thought to try this key in her door fills her mind. She snorts and shakes her head at the crazy notion, but it's annoyingly persistent.

She shrugs and figures, why the hell not? The key slides easily into the lock and when it unexpectedly clicks, she pushes forward and the door opens. Rushing inside to get out of the rain, she grabs the key and shuts the door before she stops just inside, shaking the water off of her and wringing out her hair. After a moment, she looks around in confusion and wonders why her mind is playing such tricks on her. She's in a beautifully decorated foyer, cream wallpaper with gold swirls, a travertine floor, and two huge golden double doors across from her.

The key picks up with its activity again; it's warm in her palm and, as though by a magnetic force, her hand extends to a lock on one of the doors with an etching depicting the item in her hand. It unlocks the door, and she pulls hard until it opens enough for her to slip through the crack. Only to find herself, once again, being bombarded by rain, drenching her from head to toe, her dress becoming plastered to her skin as wind whips around her. Looking back, she wants to punch something because the damn doors are no longer there. With a defeated droop in her shoulders, she trudges forward, up to yet another set of doors. Only . . . this time, they are eerily familiar. These are—she's at the front entrance of Dylan's palace. She closes her eyes and drops her head back, ready for a freak out to hit her at any minute. But, it never comes. Instead she simply wants to get out of the storm, get dry, and rest. Lifting her head back up, this is when she realizes she no longer has the key, but it really doesn't matter, no way would she walk right into Dylan's house. Even on the off chance that it would transport her to yet another random place. She takes hold of the ginormous door knocker and bangs it three times. To her relief, it doesn't take long for someone to answer.

Henry, the castle butler, sees her and gasps, immediately taking her arm and gently drawing her into the entryway. "Princess Odette! What are you doing out in this deluge?" he asks with compassion in his tone. It warms her and she finds she doesn't feel quite so cold and desolate.

"I—" She pauses, not sure how to explain without earning herself a trip to the attic to hang with Mr. Rochester's crazy-eyed wife. "It's a long story," she says, following Henry into the kitchen where he indicates she should stay and then hurries out of the room. He quickly returns with a stack of fluffy, blue towels and puts one around her shoulders, handing her a second to soak up some of the water in her hair.

"You shouldn't be out in this weather, Princess." He admonishes without real censure. "I'll make you a warm cup of tea. Is Dylan aware you were coming?" He busies himself puttering around, making her hot drink and making a plate of mouthwatering snacks.

"I don't think so." At least, since she hadn't planned to be here herself, she assumed he hadn't, either. Henry nods and shuffles over to a panel on the wall between two tall pantries. He presses a button and waits until a tinny voice comes through the speaker.

"What's up, Henry?" Odette's heart begins to pitter patter at the sound of Dylan's low timbre. His voice never fails to get her hot and bothered and this instance is no different. She squeezes her thighs together and feels her cheeks heat, hoping Henry doesn't notice her aroused state. She's also a little surprised to hear Dylan answer, he still doesn't live at the castle, so it was unlikely he would be here.

"Princess Odette is here. She was soaked through from the rain, so I brought her to the kitchen to dry off and have a hot drink," Henry informs him matter-of-factly.

"What the fuck?" Dylan growls. "Why was she out in this shit storm?"—there's a beat of silence—"never mind. I'll be right down." Henry nods, clearly satisfied with Dylan's response and finishes up the tea, bringing it to a small wooden table situated by a large fireplace.

"Have a seat, Princess," he instructs and Odette obeys without question, gratefully accepting the mug of steaming liquid. Her teeth had just begun to chatter. She sighs as she sips it and it heats her from the inside out.

"Hey, sweet pea," Dylan says as he strolls into the room. Despite the endearment and soft tone, his lips are turned down into a frown. He stops in front of her and squats down to look in her eyes. "Look at you. You're going to catch pneumonia." Taking a fresh towel from the stack, he helps to squeeze the moisture from her hair, concern in his beautiful blue eyes, currently the color of a stormy ocean, indicating his displeasure. "Why were you out in this weather, sweet pea?"

"I—um..." She gulps, trying to come up with a viable reason. "I needed to see you."

Concern darkens his eyes further. "Is everything ok?"

She nods quickly. "Nothing is wrong. I just—I needed to see you, feel you hold me."

His expression softens, and he leans forward to kiss her lips. "You know I always want to see you, Odette, but you couldn't wait until the weather cleared?"

She opens her mouth to respond but is cut off by a haughty, extremely unwelcome presence. "Odette," the queen sneers, managing to do so with a fake smile. "What has you traipsing about in weather that no lady should be out in?"

"Hello," Odette grits in acknowledgment, but she keeps her eyes on Dylan. "Can I shower and change into something dry?"

He cups one side of her face in a big palm and kisses the tip of her nose. "Of course, sweet pea. Since I'm staying here for a couple of weeks while my place is under construction, I brought some of our clean clothes over." Standing, he extends a hand and she grasps it, allowing him to pull her up, then he unceremoniously sweeps her up into his arms

"I'm getting you all wet," she admonishes even as her arms circle his neck and she rests her head on his shoulder. He brushes his lips sweetly across her forehead.

Quietly, only loud enough for Odette to hear, he whispers, "I guess, I'll have to shower with you. But, I'd prepare yourself to get even wetter." She shivers at the promise in his velvety voice. Then, to his mother, he says at regular volume, "Goodnight, Mother."

They are almost out the door when she calls out and Odette hides her grimace by burying her face in Dylan's neck. "I'll have Bernadette make up the guest room."

He stops and the muscles of his neck tense against her face as he twists his head to look at his mother over his other shoulder. "No need. Odette will be in my suite." There is a subtle bite to his tone.

"When you are king, you may sleep with whomever you

like, Dylan," she states in a frosty tone. "Until then, your . . . friend . . . sleeps in a guest room." Her deliberate exclusion of "girl" before friend doesn't go unnoticed. The hardening of Dylan's jaw has Odette doing a mental fist bump. Because mentally giving her the bird isn't very princessy and she was determined to prove the old bat wrong, even if it was only in her head.

"Fine," he says tightly and Odette's head whips up, almost busting his chin. But, when she looks up, he winks at her. "I'll put her in the rose guest room."

"Well, I was going to prepare the yel—" She starts to argue with him but he quickly shuts her down.

"—My room or the rose room, Mother."

She sniffs haughtily and Odette rolls her eyes. "The rose room is reserved for princesses, Dylan."

Odette's jaw drops. King father, queen mother, eleven princess sisters . . . *pretty sure it qualifies me as a princess, you old biddy.*

"Another reason to put Odette in there, Mother," Dylan tosses out flippantly as he strides from the kitchen.

Odette lays her head back down, muttering, *"Does she think I was spawned by the milkman?"* He laughs as he treks through the castle until they reach his suite of rooms, but stops at the door in the hall right before the entrance to his bedroom. Letting her legs go, he gently helps her to stand steadily on her feet. Keeping his hands on her waist, he turns her around to face the room, then shuffles her inside. It's gorgeous, decorated in varying shades of rose and grey.

Dylan dips his head to the side of hers and points to a door, he murmurs, "See the door there?" She nods. "As it happens, it opens up to my bedroom." His next words are practically purred. "Now, don't go getting any lascivious ideas, sweet pea." He nibbles on her ear and the pitter patter of her heart returns. "Let me show you the bathroom."

Stepping away, he takes her hand and she trails behind him when he leaves the room and enters the next door down. This room is clearly masculine, done in creams, chocolate brown, and a hint of light grey. He continues across the room and enters a gorgeous bathroom with a shower big enough to fit at least six people. It sits in the center of the room, all for walls made of glass, the erotic images suddenly filling her head heat her up more than the tea had.

Dylan shuts the door and walks over to the shower, turning it on before returning to where she is standing aimlessly. Without a word, he begins to undress her, his fingers leaving goosebumps in their wake. If she wasn't already drenched from head to toe, she might have been a little embarrassed by how wet she is between her legs. Her dress unbuttons in the front and he makes quick work of it, then kneels down to help her step out of it before kissing his way back up, pausing to lick through her slick folds. "Hmm, seems you aren't just soaked from the rain, sweet pea." Odette moans, incapable of speech, shivering for an entirely different reason. "I'm not happy you were out in this dangerous weather, especially making the six-hour drive from Rêves, however"—he reached her breasts and stops to lick each hardened nipple—"I'm very happy you are here." He stands, and she gets to watch him discard his own clothes, showing off his spectacular physique.

Picking her up again, he takes them both to the glass enclosure, now fogged up with steam. He steps inside and under the spray of four different shower heads, then lets her wet body slide slowly down, letting her feel everything, all of him. His eyes are deep grey-blue now, filled with flames of desire, and a sexy smile on his face. She grabs him by the back of his neck and tugs him down to kiss him, moaning when he eagerly participates. He nips at her, sweeps his tongue inside, and sucks her bottom lip into his mouth. She flinches when she suddenly finds her herself backed up to the cold glass, and she bites Dylan's lip when he chuckles.

"Ouch, sweet pea," he pouts, running his tongue over the abused spot. "Be nice, or you're going to get yourself in trouble."

She perks up curiously. "What kind of trouble?"

He narrows his eyes, his hands roaming up to cup her breasts before pinching her nipples hard enough to make her yelp. "The kind where you get a spanking and get fucked hard and rough up against the wall of my shower."

Odette's heart is pounding and her pussy clenches, suddenly gushing with arousal. She gets close to him again in a half a second and bites his lip hard enough to draw a little blood. Dylan growls and pulls her away from the wall before his hand lands on her ass with a ringing slap. She gasps as the sting of pain and the accompanying streak of pleasure. He gives her other cheek the same treatment. Alternating so each gets three hard smacks.

She whimpers and before she knows it, Dylan has the glass supporting her back as he puts her legs around his waist and drives his cock into her pussy, fully seating himself in one thrust. "Oh fuck!" he shouts in ecstasy and freezes, every muscle tight, his face contorted as he tries to regain control of himself. The walls of her pussy clench around his big, long cock, earning her another spanking. "Behave," he growls, starting to slowly move in and out.

"Make me," she pants sassily as she bears down once more.

"Odette!" he yells, but it ends on a deep groan and his hips pick up triple the speed, going so deep he bumps her womb every time.

"Yes, Dylan! Harder!" she screams, close, so close to coming.

"I should go slow and torture you," he scolds tightly, his jaw flexed from clenching his teeth. "Lucky for you, I haven't fucked you in two months and I need you fast and hard."

He pounds into her, her screams making him more and more frantic with his thrusts, plunging deep inside without rhythm, lost to his senses. "Oh fuck, oh fuck. Damn, sweet pea, I need you to come. Your pussy is milking me, and I'm not going to last much longer," he grinds out. "Come now, Odette." He lifts her under the ass and bends his knees slightly so she is falling down on his cock and after two drops, she flies apart, creaming on his cock, making her pussy so slick he slides easily in and out, despite the grip of her walls.

He raises her up and drops her down on his cock one, two, three more times, then he shoves her back against the wall and shouts as he buries himself so deep she feels his hot come explode, coating her womb. Over and over, jets of semen burst from him, and each time, it sets her off on another mini-orgasm. His bruising grip on her ass and the pressure with which he's got her backed against the glass, keeps their groins plastered together so nothing escapes.

Later, they are completely lethargic from rounds two and three before they finally washed and finished their shower. He tells her to stay put while he gets her something to wear, so she waits by the half-open door of the bathroom.

There is a knock on his door and he makes a low noise of frustration as he throws on a pair of pajama pants and strides over to open it. He crosses his arms across his defined chest and leans casually against the door frame, keeping the door mostly closed behind him.

"Mother. What do you need?"

"She's in there with you." His mother's accusatory voice carries clearly to where Odette is waiting.

"There is no need to point out something I already know. Get to the point, mother," he says with a sigh.

"You can't marry her, Dylan. She's not a real princess."

"For the love of . . . what the hell are you talking about?"

She sniffs, "Watch your language, young man."

"I'm sorry." His voice holds genuine remorse, but there is still a hard edge to it. "I don't know how you've convinced yourself of this, but what is it going to take to dispel this absurd notion?" Odette tenses, waiting to hear what the crazy woman has come up with.

"I've added several mattresses to her bed. We'll put something small under the lowest one. If she's really a princess, she won't be able to sleep because she'll feel it."

Odette covers her mouth in a bid not to laugh hysterically, but it turns out to not be necessary when she realizes Dylan is taking it seriously. "Fine," he gruffs, "I'll take care of it, and we'll see you in the morning."

"She has to sleep there alone, Dylan. Otherwise, your restlessness from the item will keep her awake anyway. Not that you were planning to sleep with her, I'm sure. I'm sure you want to make your mother happy."

Dylan doesn't say anything but Odette swears she can hear his eyes roll. He moves out of her line of vision and there is another beat of silence. He must be giving her a kiss on the cheek, then he says, "Goodnight, Mother." Odette clearly hears the sound of her patting his face, as though he was a child. *Oh, brother.*

She steps back and waits for the door to shut and Dylan's steps back to the bathroom. He pushes the door open and smiles, holding out a t-shirt and a pair of his boxer briefs. "Here, sweet pea, as much as I'd love to keep you just as you are, I've already fucked you senseless in my mother's house. I suppose we can give her something and sleep apart." His eyes darken and he steps close. "You never sleep naked unless you're in bed with me, is that clear?"

"Okay," she says, agreeing easily because she doesn't like to sleep naked unless she's plastered up against his warm skin.

He grins and pecks her on the nose. "Good girl." He shows her to the other room again, both of them pretending the stack of mattresses is the most natural thing in the world. She climbs up after he turns her to jelly with a scorching kiss, then he leaves, turning off the light and shutting the connecting door.

She shifts around, trying to detect where the "something" is, but she isn't able to find it. She begins to wonder—*no!* Punching her pillow in annoyance, she flops down and goes to sleep. Later, half awake, she shifts to try and get comfortable; it felt like something was digging into her back. It was a very painful, fitful night's sleep.

Dylan sits on the ground, back against the wall, and his long legs stretched out in front of him as he watches Odette sleep. He'd driven all night to be here in the morning, unable to wait any longer. After he'd arrived, he'd sat down, fallen asleep, and had the weirdest, yet sexiest dream... Content to enjoy the beauty before him, he knows he made the right choice. There had been a plan, an elaborate, amazing, thoroughly romantic plan, but he was impatient and done trying to hide things from the love of his life. He'd informed his mother last night that he was going to propose to Odette and she needed to get on board. In order to be a part of her grandchildren's lives, she needed to respect their mother and treat her kindly. He'd saved the threat for extreme measures, and it had been necessary, gaining her instantaneous agreement, as he knew it would.

He was already in the car when he'd received a call from Odette's twin, Shelby. She was worried about Odette, who'd been so upset by everything, she was making herself sick. He quizzed Shelby for a good ten minutes, making her detail exactly what she was talking about. The thought that his woman had been in such a state of stress, she was getting sick, had a rock settling in the pit of his stomach. As Shelby talked, something in the back of his mind was trying to get to the surface, but he couldn't get a grasp on it. A few minutes later, it hit him like a ton of bricks and his face cracked into a wide and ecstatic smile. It hadn't left his face since then.

Odette shifts restlessly in her sleep, tossing and turning, unable to get comfortable until finally, she groans and sits up. She rubs her lower back and glares down at the mattress, then realizes there is a lump under her mattress pad. She huffs and climbs out of bed, stomping on the floor and she puts her feet down. She bends over, incidentally, giving Dylan a fantastic view of her very appealing ass.

Reaching under the pad, she retrieves the box he'd slid underneath her fifteen minutes ago. She stares perplexedly at the blue velvet box in her hand, then lifts her head, her eyes darting all around the room until they land on him.

"Dylan?" she breathes. He grins and opens his arms wide. She scrambles over to him straightaway, straddling his legs and snuggling into his embrace.

"Hey, sweet pea." Dylan buries his face into her silky hair and inhales her sexy, citrusy scent. It calms him before he can start to get nervous. "I love you, you know that?"

She angles back so she is looking at his face with almost a shy smile. "I hope so." Her demeanor shifts a little, and he sees worry creep into her eyes. "Because, um, I have something to tell you."

He places a finger over her lips to silence her. "Me first, please?" he pleads, blinking his eyes in a way he knows she can't resist. And, sure enough, she giggles and motions for him to continue. He holds out his hand wordlessly and waits. She glances at his open palm with confusion, then, it suddenly clicks, you can almost see the lightbulb above her head turn on.

Looking at Dylan's hand warily, she clutches the box to her chest possessively. "You already gave it to me," she mutters. He laughs and can't resist a short kiss.

"I promise to give it back, as long as I like your answer."

"Why do I have to give it back for you to ask?" she pouts.

He raises a challenging eyebrow and wiggles his fingers. Huffing, she puts the box in Dylan's hand and he sneaks one more laughing kiss.

"Odette? Sweet pea?" he coos softly. She grins and wiggles impatiently on his lap. "I love you more than any man every loved a woman. I want to spend eternity with you. Marry you, have babies with you, and rule my kingdom together. Will you be the queen of my heart, my name, and my kingdom?"

"Hell, yes!" she screams and launches herself at him, kissing every thought right the fuck out of his head. When she sits back, she snatches the box, but he swipes it right back with a glower. Opening it, he takes out a necklace made from a delicate, platinum chain, holding a platinum charm shaped like a pea pod, holding three perfectly round jade balls. Hanging next to it is a charm with the words "*Sweet Pea*" inscribed.

Odette looks a little crestfallen but tries valiantly to hide it. Dylan can't keep from chuckling and her expression shifts to suspicious. "To remind everyone you're my sweet pea," he tells her as he clasps the chain around her neck. Then, he dips a finger in his pocket and pulls out an intricately weaved, white-gold band, with a three-karat, queen cut diamond perched on top, flanked on either side by a princess cut green diamond. Odette gasps as Dylan slides it onto her left ring finger. "To remind everyone you are my wife, my queen."

She throws her arms around his neck, sobbing and he frantically thinks of something to say to get her to stop crying. Logically, he knows they are happy tears, but anytime she cries, it guts him. Then, he remembers... "Sweet pea, about the baby part—" His sentence goes unfinished when she hiccups, then lurches back with her hands over her mouth. Dylan jumps to his feet with her in his arms, and races to the bathroom, getting there just in time for her to empty her stomach.

"I guess we'll have to move up the wedding date," he comments smugly. "Looks like I already got a head start on the making babies part."

Ovaries go POOM

Odette and Dylan are officially engaged (with the rock—and holy fuck is that a rock—to prove it) and having a baby. I beat back the yearning I feel coming on, screaming foul and yelling at it to get right back in the dugout. Cheeky little bitch, trying to stealthily round the bases and steal home, attempting to consume me with baby fever.

My sister is positively glowing, and I'm determined to keep my focus on her, ignoring the searing gaze burning into my back. Until I feel the heat of his body right behind me,

when he Oliver steps even closer and he slips an arm around me, pressing me up against him. His big hand splays across my belly, keeping me from moving, and his hot breath bathes my ear, sending tingles skittering down my spine. "I can't wait to see you with my baby in your belly," he confesses softly. "You're already so damn beautiful, baby. I don't know how I'm going to let you out of bed. It can only get worse once you're full of a little life we create together."

I swear; my uterus skips a beat. Then, his supple lips brush my neck and it's all I can do to stay upright. His dark chuckle tells me I'm only standing because he's holding me steady. "I can't wait to hold our little one," he whispers against my skin. Uninvited images flood my mind.

A gorgeous, black-haired baby with stunning blue eyes, in the arms of its unbelievably sexy daddy.

BOOM

Sulking, Wilhelm? Really?

OLIVER

I'm fighting with everything I have not to drag Pippa to a secluded place and fill her with me until she's knocked the fuck up. The time when I'll finally be able to let go of my tightly reined control is getting nearer. And, my body seems to know it, reminding me at any given moment how much it wants to get lost inside Pippa.

The family starts to disperse, couples pairing off and heading home, but I remain seated, with Pippa snuggled up to my side, while I'm deep in discussion with Wilder. We barely hear the doorbell ring as we work out a problem with one of the expansions.

"Wilder." We are interrupted when Wilder's partner, Phoenix, calls his name as he strides into the room and over to where we are seated. "How are you, Oliver?" he asks before his eyes stray to Pippa.

I glare at him and drag Pippa into my lap. "Doing well. I'll be even better in the next week when I'm married to *my* woman." I manage to remain simply gruff instead of snarling. Pippa stiffens in my lap and I glance down to see her glaring at me. I roll my eyes and return to my conversation with Wilder, now including Phoenix, who'd stopped by to give us an update.

I ask Phoenix a question but he doesn't answer, his eyes are trained across the room, a look I recognize coming over his face. I can't really judge considering my history with Pippa. Looks like Phoenix is going to get his fantasy girl tonight. *Lucky bastard.* Shelby catches his gaze and blushes profusely, pushing her glasses up her pert nose, while Wilhelm does a little jig in my pocket. *Yeah, yeah, brother Grimm, keep your panties on.* The snotty little shock doesn't even faze me anymore. Wilhelm pulses once more before going silent again. Is he...? *Are you sulking, Wilhelm?*

I hold in a sigh, not only am I talking to a key, I'm talking to a magical key with an attitude. Is this what crazy looks like? Pippa shifts on my lap, surreptitiously snuggling a little closer. Maybe crazy looks better than I thought.

Phoenix wanders over to where Shelby is chatting with her mother and Piper. He speaks to all three of them, but then he and Shelby pair off, quietly talking. I'm only half paying attention to Wilder and don't even notice when he gets up and collects Piper and leaves.

"Goodnight, Wilder. Later, twinkles," Pippa says as she scoots off my lap. Not wanting to be any ruder, I stand to say goodbye to the departing couple. After they leave, Pippa covertly peers back and forth between me and the door, clearly not sure whether she wants to stay or go. It's late, and I need to get the key to Shelby before she takes off, so I make the decision for her. Wrapping her up in my arms, I kiss her with passion until the clearing of a throat reminds me where we are. I glance up at her mother guiltily, but she's shaking her head at us, chuckling. I grin back at her and give Pippa one more squeeze before letting her loose.

"Goodnight, ladies." I slowly amble towards the front entrance to the castle, prolonging my journey, hoping I won't have to wait around like a creepy stalker. Wilhelm hums. *Over your snit, are you?*

I'm at the door when I hear the sound of approaching voices and I remove Wilhelm from my pocket and linger, ostensibly waiting for Phoenix. Calling out to him when they come around the corner to cement the assumption.

"Going back the office, Phoenix?"

He glances at Shelby and shakes his head. "No, Shelby is going to show me some of her finds from her trip." He gestures for her to precede him, "Shall we?"

I hold the door open and when Shelby walks by, I slip the key into her purse. She smiles up at me, then I shake Phoenix's hand, and we all descend the steps together, get in our cars, and go our separate ways.

This time, when I go to bed, I dream about my beautiful Pippa rounded with a swollen belly, and a dark-haired, green-eyed little girl holding her hand as they advance towards me.

Meanwhile...

Shelby's Fantasy

WHERE THE FUCK ARE MY SEASHELLS?

Shelby unlocks the door to her lab and flicks on the lights, leading the way in, very aware of the man following her. She takes a deep breath to fortify her hormones before facing him again.

"This was a Spanish excavation. Some of the items we found show the signs of being from an undiscovered people." She smiles and gestures for him to take a seat on a stool at a long, illuminated lab table. Her mind races, trying to think of what the most interesting pieces and facts are for her to share. People often glaze over when she starts to talk about her work, unless it's about buried pirate treasure. She didn't have any of those stories—yet. Hopefully, someday.

She returns to the table with a tray of items she'd recently catalogued and assigned to a display at a museum in Madrid. Gauging his expression, to see if she's boring him, she points to each piece and explains their origin. He listens raptly, making her feel like the most fascinating person he's ever met. "Anyway, this is the project I'm working on right now."

He nods, studying her thoughtfully. "When do you leave again?"

Shrugging as she puts everything away, she muses, "I'm not sure. This is a big job and with my degree, they wanted me to be in charge of the land project, too." When she comes back to the table, he's frowning at her and it makes her stomach dip. What had she said?

"Then you'll leave again? For how long?" he asks, his expression becoming more along the lines of frustration. "You were gone for a little over sixteen months last time?"

"Well, yes, but that's because I chose to stay with this crew for several projects," she explains carefully, wishing he'd go back to smiling at her. "There really isn't a way to know how long a project or hunt will take. With this load, though, the site had already been discovered and our time on the water was actually pretty limited. We were brought in to help excavate and finish up with the tedious archeological stuff." She smiles ruefully and points at her chest with her thumb. "Enter, Shelby."

Phoenix rubs a hand over his brown goatee, showing hints of red in the light. His brows are still furrowed, but he's softened his features. "Thank you, suga—Shelby," he says, stumbling over her name. "This is amazing, the work you do. I appreciate you sharing it with me." He stands up and comes around the table. When he leans in, Shelby sucks in a breath and closes her eyes, sure he's about to kiss her. She feels the whisper soft brush of his lips on her cheek and then the heat of his body in front of her is replaced by cool air as he steps back. Opening her eyes, she darts her gaze to the ground, horribly embarrassed at reading him so wrong.

He lifts her chin with a finger and smiles. "You're incredible, Shelby. Smart, funny, so beautiful it almost hurts to look at you." She senses the but ahead and is disappointed to be right. "I have a business here, it's my home. I can't start a relationship with someone who is going to be leaving me for undeterminable amounts of time, multiple times a year. And,

I would never want to hold you back, to be the reason you didn't go after your dreams." He falls quiet, looking as though he debating saying something else, but all he says is, "Goodnight, sugar." Then he walks out, shutting the door behind him, the click of the lock echoing in the silence.

Shelby sighs and sits at the lab table, slumping over, and resting her chin on her folded arms. At least he didn't leave her because he thought she was boring. She'd only ever been out on one date, most guys dismissing her before even giving her a chance. The one date had turned out to be a guy whose only goal was to get in her wetsuit. She'd given him a black eye when he'd attempted to cop a feel.

Getting to her feet, she turns the lights off and opens the door . . . Except, it doesn't budge. *Stupid doors.* These doors don't unlock, they are either kept open, or you have to use a key to get in and out of the room. Irritated at, everything and everyone, she digs through her purse for her keys. They don't seem to be there and she glances around not seeing them lying around anywhere. Damn it. She takes her glasses off and rubs her eyes. *Shelby, the absentminded professor strikes again.*

A dull noise in her purse draws her attention and she opens it, startled to see and odd, gold skeleton key. Where did this come from? Had Phoenix put it in there? Some untold force draws her eyes to the door of the lab. She puts her glasses back on and notices a light shining through the keyhole. Which is weird since the window in the door shows an empty, unlit hallway.

It makes no sense whatsoever to try the skeleton key, but it's almost as if it has a mind of its own, guiding her to the lock. It works. *Holy shit, it worked?* Turns out, that's not the end of the peculiar events currently happening. She steps into a marvelous foyer and turns in a circle, soaking up the richness of the space. There are two large, gold-brushed doors and she decides she might as well jump head first into whatever universe she suddenly finds herself in. Taking the key from the door she'd entered through, she sticks it in a lock, bearing a carving of the very key in her hand.

She figures it must be her sense of adventure and discovery pushing her to keep going and has a fleeting thought of caution, but ignores it in favor of hope that there's nothing on the other side of the door that would eat her.

Opening it, she's hit by a wall of water. It sucks her into its depths, filling her mouth and nose, causing her to choke and swallow water into her lungs. *Maybe being eaten by a giant whale wouldn't be such a bad thing, right now.* Her panic capriciously dissipates and she relaxes, now considering whether she ingested too many fumes in her lab and is hallucinating, because there is no way she's breathing underwater. No way at all.

Looking around, she forgets about her weird predicament and gets lost in the maritime world, the place she feels most at home. She kicks her legs to propel her forward and goes hurtling much, much faster than she should have. When she slows, she takes the opportunity to scrutinize herself. If she'd been standing, she probably would have fainted. Then again, with these fins, she wouldn't have been standing anyway. Yup, that's right—fins. Turns out, she's a fucking mermaid.

Shelby shakes her head and tries to dislocate whatever organism has crawled into her brain and laid crazy eggs. It doesn't work. With a sigh, she decides to head for the surface, hoping fresh air will be the trick. She allows herself to revel in the swim, the rush of the cool water over her skin as she speeds to the surface, the sounds of the ocean filling her ears in a way it never could before. *Okay, so this mermaid thing isn't so bad.*

Forgetting to slow her speed as she gets closer to the top, she breaks through the water and goes hurtling into the sky. She freaks out for about thirty seconds until she remembers to go with the flow (pun intended) and does a graceful arc before diving back into the water. She smirks to herself, wondering if she should dye her hair red. "Ahhhh . . . ahhh . . . ahhhhhha . . . aahhh." Not so much with the singing, though. She coughs and chokes a little, the salt making her throat scratchy, but at least she can still breathe.

Coming to the surface at a more sedate pace this time, she floats, with her fin moving lazily to keep her upright. *Definitely getting the hang of the fins for feet situation.* The wind picks up a little and she shivers as her nipples pebble and point. What??? Glancing down, she groans in exasperation. *Where the fuck are my seashells?* And, since life is like a rotten box of chocolates, this is the moment she notices the row boat coming upon her.

Mortified, she sinks down, trying to cover her bare breasts but strike number one for the fins; she's floating like a buoy. There has to be a way to force herself to sink, right? *Too late.*

"Hey! Are you crazy? What are you doing swimming out here alone in the middle of the fucking ocean?" A voice yells. It also sends tingles racing down to her ... hmm. Exactly how does that work? Disney certainly never explained the Mer birds and bees. "Hello?"

Shelby crosses her arms over her naked chest and rotates in the water until she's facing the owner of the tingle-inducing voice. She gasps and heat flushes through her body, the blush more than likely showing up all over her exposed skin. It's Phoenix. In the boat. On the ocean. Phoenix. Staring at her, oh! Oops, in her shock, she'd let her arms go lax for a minute there. Covering up once again, it breaks his line of sight to her breasts, and he seems to realize he was ogling her. In the moonlight, she can see pink tinging his cheeks as he meets her gaze.

His eyes are a beautiful, deep green, and his thick, black lashes, brush the apples of his cheeks when he blinks at her. After a minute, she realizes he doesn't recognize her and she can't quite tamp down a stem of hurt. Sure, she's a fish, but the upper body still looks the same, other than the lack of clothing.

The boat sidles up next to her, and he smiles, taking her breath away. *Wow.* He's lethal with that weapon. "What's your name, sugar?"

She opens her mouth to answer and starts coughing again, the salt had stuck to the inside of her throat and dried it out. A whisper of sound is all she can manage and it's completely useless. He frowns with worry and reaches for her. "Let me help you into the boat. I can't just leave you here and even if there were someone else to help you, you've lost your voice and can't call for them."

Shelby instinctively shimmies away then she sinks. Yup, right down into the suddenly frigid ocean water and her next inhale causes more choking, her lungs burning. The next thing she knows, she's being dragged up from the water and tossed over the side of the dinghy. The boat dips as Phoenix hauls himself over the side.

She sucks in a huge lungful of air repeatedly, spitting out water and shivering in the cold. A blanket falls in her lap and she looks up into angry green pools. "I'm not sure if you're crazy or truly talented at playing the damsel in distress, but either way, keep your ass planted right in that spot while I take us back to the ship." He sits on a bench and shakes the water out of his hair before picking up the oars. Her teeth start to chatter, and he gives her a sharp look. "Cover up before you freeze to death," he growls.

Amidst all of this, she's wondering why he hasn't mentioned anything about the small detail of, oh yeah, she's part fish. Bending her knees, she wraps the blanket around her shoulders and is about to close it when she realizes she is, in fact, staring at real knees. Human knees. Cold and tired, she decides not to dwell on it. *Go with the flow, Shelby.*

It takes almost an hour for him to row them to a large, old-fashioned, pirate ship. Nothing about this night is going to surprise her anymore, so she simply sighs and takes Phoenix's hand when he lends it to help her stand. Then, he unceremoniously tosses her over his shoulder and starts climbing up the ladder to the ship deck.

Once they are on the relatively solid ground, he sets her down and closes the blanket tightly around her, glaring at every man who looks their way. He scoops her up, into his arms this time, and takes her to the captain's quarters and lays her on the bed. Standing back, hands on his hips, he scrutinizes her with a fierce scowl. She squirms under his hot stare and, now that she is inconveniently without a fin, she feels her pussy flood with arousal.

Her eyes stray to his . . . are those, breeches? Hmmm, they certainly make the bulge of what must be an enormous cock, hard and ready to go, a lot more obvious. Then again, "conveniently" seems like a much better choice of word at this very moment. He growls, and her eyes fly back up to meet his, the green almost glowing with the fire burning in them. "If you don't stop looking at me like that, you're going to find yourself fucked into next week, sugar."

She opens her mouth to deny it staring, then remembers her lack of voice. She mentally shrugs it as a lie anyway. In this instant, she makes a rare, bold decision. This is clearly a dream, or high, or alternate universe, but whatever it is, she's going to make the best of it. Doing her best to give him a sultry look, she tosses the blanket away and lies out on the bed like an offering.

Phoenix's eyes widen to the size of saucers and his jaw drops, but he's also breathing erratically, his pulse pounding so hard she can see it in his neck. "You don't know what you're asking for, sugar. I suggest you get under those covers and try to get some rest."

She starts to argue with him, tell him she knows exactly what she wants, but there is no sound. Ugh! This mute thing sucks! Next time she watches *The Little Mermaid*, she'll have a little more empathy for Ariel. Her only recourse is to show him then. Scooting to the edge of the bed, she palms his cock through his pants, smiling smugly when he hisses and his hips thrust into her hand.

Fifteen seconds later, she's flat on her back, naked, covered by the sexiest man she's ever met, and being kissed like she's the answer to world hunger. After about ten minutes of making out like teenagers, he raises his head and stares down at her, his face full of wonder.

"Who are you?" he muses aloud, knowing he won't be able to get an actual answer. "I feel as though I've known you for my whole life. Longer than that even." He kisses her again, a long, slow, drugging kiss. "You know I'm going to take you now, right?" he asks, probing her face with his eyes. She nods and lifts her hips to let him know she's completely amenable to this plan. He stills her by pressing her into the bed, still serious and brooding. "Let me be very clear, sugar. I'm going to take you and then you are going to be mine. *Mine.*" He emphasizes the last word through a clamped jaw. At this point, she'd give him whatever the hell he wants if he would simply follow up all these words with some freaking action!

His mouth slams down over hers and she sighs in relief, even as her heart rate picks up, and walls of her pussy spasm in anticipation. Despite how subtle the tensing of her muscles are, he must notice because he groans and grinds his erection into the V of her thighs, where he's resting his weight. She moans in response, and he nips at her lip before journeying down to lap and suck on her nipples, a little bite here and there, too. She writhes beneath him as he tortures her until she is so worked up, if she were able to talk, she'd be screaming and cussing him out, demanding he let her come. As it is though, she has no other choice but to take what he gives her. It's a win either way, really.

He moves down even further and Shelby feels the need to recant her earlier thought about not being eaten. Her voice suddenly has reappearance, allowing her to scream her opinion right before she comes violently, her body rocking with hard shudders. She's still in an orgasm induced coma when Phoenix returns to the bed, and she realizes he'd gotten up and stripped naked.

"No turning back now, sugar," he growls. "You're mine and when I've fucked you so full of come that you are carrying my baby, everyone else will know it, too."

There is no time for her to even process what he says, much less respond to it, before he drives inside, his cock stretching her pussy from its size. She sucks in a breath at the pain of losing her virginity and he freezes. "Damn it, sugar. I'm so sorry, I should have asked if this as your first time." His voice is as thick with apology as it with lust, but he manages to give her a sheepish grin. "It's not like you could have told me on your own." Shifting a centimeter to test the fit, he raises his brows at her. "Still hurt?"

"No," she manages to croak out. "Feels..." She can't get out any more words but she bucks her hips up in answer.

His grins become a smile filled with dark, passionate promises. They fuck hard, knocking the headboard against the wall (this is a huge accomplishment, considering the bed is bolted to the floor) before coming together, shouting their release. Eventually, they collapse in an exhausted, but satisfied heap.

Phoenix rolls to his back, taking her with him so she lies atop him, their bodies still connected. "Shelby?" he whispers out of the blue.

She swiftly rises up, supporting herself with her elbows on

his chest. "Yes," she confirms, her voice stronger and less scratchy. "How do you know that?"

He shrugs and brushes a lock of her hair behind her ear. "I don't know. But, since I first saw you in the water, I've known two things. You were made to be mine, and I was instantly, irrevocably in love with you. Learning your name was just a perk."

Shelby's heart practically grows wings and takes flight. "You love me?" Her voice is strong and fully restored.

"More than I thought it was possible to love another person, sugar," he murmurs, love shining in the emerald green depths of his eyes.

"Me too," she whispers.

Phoenix comes awake with a start and falls off the chair he's sitting in. He looks around in a daze, wondering where the hell he's at. It slowly starts to trickle back; the white walls, ugly maroon carpet, and the smell of the ocean. He's at Shelby's lab. After he left her, he realized he couldn't leave her here alone this late at night, so he took a seat in sitting area directly across from the door to her room.

Taking a gander at his watch, he sees it's just past four in the morning. Fuck! He hoped she hadn't slipped out and left him sleeping. It wasn't safe for her to be walking out to her car alone in the darkness. He rubs the sleep from his eyes and gets to his feet, wincing when he feels the stiffness in his groin. His dreams about Shelby were erotic as fuck. But more than that, they made him admit what he'd been denying.

Finally, on his feet and fully awake, he rushes over to the door and tries to open it. It's locked, but some of his tension releases when he sees Shelby through the window, asleep at her lab table. He starts knocking urgently, but not too hard, afraid to scare her awake.

After a couple of minutes, she stirs and sits up, looking adorably mussed and disoriented. He knocks a little harder to draw her attention his way, then points down to the door handle. Shelby slowly climbs off the stool, roots around in her purse before pulling out a set of keys and pads over to the door. She unlocks it, and he opens it in such a rush, she goes hurtling into his arms.

"Ooph!" she grunts as the wind gets knocked out of her.

"Sorry, sugar," he says gently. "I was a little over anxious." Her head lifts and that's when he sees the dried tear stains on her enchanting face. His heart starts to hurt, afraid he knows why she was crying. "You've been crying," he states with a regretful sigh.

"I thought you—we—that there was something—" He kisses her, effectively silencing her explanation. He was right, she'd been crying because he hurt her. Now he needed to fix it, and he would do it by being honest with her and himself.

"Shelby, when I first saw you last night, you knocked me on my proverbial ass. Did you know that?" he asks with a crooked smile. She shakes her head and watches him warily. "There were two things which hit me like a ton of bricks."

"Two things?" she repeats, her eyes growing.

He nods. "Two things. One, you were made to be mine and two—"

"You were instantly, irrevocably in love with me," she finishes for him.

They stare at each other in shock. She breaks the spell with a shrug, dismissing the weirdness of the moment. "You still left. Why are you here now?"

He tentatively sets his lips on hers, pleased when she doesn't retreat and lets him kiss her. Breaking apart, he drops his eyes to the ground awkwardly. "I left because I was being a selfish fucking coward, sugar," he admits. "I thought if I didn't have you in the first place, it would make it easier to give you up. It took an instant for me to fall for you, an hour for me to act like a jackass and fuck it up, and about two minutes for me to realize I was wrong."

"So, what happens now?" she frets. It's clear he doing a shit job of explaining.

"Now, I make plans to be with you, wherever you go, whenever you go, whatever it takes. I'll be with you."

It feels as tough a cache of rocks lifts off his chest when her face breaks into a smile. "If you had asked, I would have told you I was mostly content to stay here and work. I want to be with you, to start a family, and have stability. I would still like to go out on a project, perhaps once a year, for no longer than a month. My thought was, maybe you and our children could go with me. Spend one month of every year traveling and discovering the world together."

Phoenix is staring at Shelby in fascination, his heart about to explode with love. "Sugar," he breathes, "you're fucking brilliant!"

How about that, Mr. Doubting Mustafa?

OLIVER

The bell over the door jingles as I enter a small jewelry store downtown. The young, blonde clerk looks up and smiles with a blush. "Where can I find Sabrina?" I ask curtly, looking for Pippa's sister. I don't want to be rude, but I don't like the way she is looking me and I don't want to give her the impression she has a shot. She points down a hallway, and I nod my thanks before heading in that direction.

"Hi, Oliver!" Sabrina waves at me from through the open door to her workshop. She's wearing protective gear and holding a small welding torch. She sets if down carefully and removes her gloves before giving me a hug. "It's all done. Do you want to see it?" She beams at me and I must look as eager as I feel because she laughs and trots over to an old, steel safe.

Sabrina is a jewelry maker, not in the typical sense, like what you see in a store at the mall. Her pieces are practically art and they sell all over the world, especially in the United States. I was having Pippa's ring made, and I didn't want to give it to her in the generic little jewelry box it would be given to me in. So, I went to Sabrina with an idea and she'd executed it. Removing a black, velvet bag, she comes back over to the table and shakes the contents out into her hand.

The locket is shaped like a book, only large enough to fit an engagement ring. It's made of a kaleidoscope of colored quartz, and hanging from a platinum chain. Each side of the little "book" is inscribed. One side says, *The greatest love story of all*, and the other says, *Was the day I fell in love with you*.

"It's perfect, Sabrina," I compliment her, a little in awe of her talent.

"I hope you get to use it soon." She sighs and I cast her a questioning glance. "I'm not likely to find love anytime soon," she elaborates, her eyes suddenly turning sad. There is a story there, I'm sure of it. It's quickly one and she winks at me. "I have faith in your powers of persuasion."

"You never know. Love may find you when you least expect it," I suggest.

She eyes me doubtfully. "Maybe. Well, I'd better get back to work. I have a client coming to pick up this piece tomorrow." She walks purposefully back to her work table and my eye catches on her current project. I follow her to get a closer look at it.

"Is that an oil lamp?" I ask, studying the gold object, its shape, and the etchings all over it. She nods distractedly as she picks up an engraving pen. "As in Aladdin's magic lamp? The one with the genie?" I'm laughing by the time I finish my question.

Sabrina chuckles along with me. "I just make what they ask, I don't always understand it."

Just then her assistant calls her name and she excuses herself to go and see what she needs. I'm still inspecting the beautiful lamp when I feel Wilhelm making a racket in my pocket. *It's Sabrina's turn, huh?* He vibrates faster, giving me my answer. Sabrina and Abbi are twins; the last two Wilhelm has to pair off. I wasn't sure which would be first, but now that I know it's Sabrina, I start looking around for the perfect place to leave the key.

My eyes land on the lamp again and Wilhelm hums. It's as a good a place as any, I suppose. She'll find it when she goes to put the piece away tonight. Carefully, so as to not do any damage to the delicate lamp, I lower Wilhelm into it. The top is on the table and I deliberate whether or not to close the lamp. Ultimately, I decide to leave it. If I leave right now, she won't find it while I'm here, even if she should discover it right away after coming back to her workshop. I turn towards the door but my feet turn to lead and I can't seem to go any further. Standing there, I try and talk myself out of it, but I'm not successful. My feet are no longer glued to the ground when I pivot and sidle up to the lamp. I roll my eyes at myself, flabbergasted at what I'm about to do. It can't hurt, though, right?

Stretching my arm out, I call myself ten different kinds of an idiot as my hand touches the cool metal. Yep. If you're thinking I rubbed the lamp and made a wish, I'm sorry to tell you your assumption is correct. Go ahead. Laugh. Just don't ever tell Pippa.

Beating a hasty retreat, I wave to Sabrina on my way out the door and take my ridiculous self home. I arrive and get comfortable, then park my ass where it always seems to be in the evenings, on the couch with a glass of scotch. I'm trying not to dwell on the lamp, but I wonder if Sabrina will have more luck and a big, blue genie will help her find her true love.

Meanwhile...

Sabrina's Fantasy

HOP ON MY FLYING CARPET, ANGEL

Standing back, Sabrina admires her work. The lamp really did turn out beautiful, and she's excited to show it her client. She picks it up and carries it over to a locked cage where she keeps her larger, finished pieces. Tilting it so she can get it under the top lip of the shelf, she hears a clunk from inside the lamp. Her eyes scan the piece in panic, looking for anything that could have broken off and fallen inside. The handle, lid, and spout seem unharmed and the rest of the lamp is smooth and unadorned except for the etchings.

The lamp begins to vibrate in her hands. What in the world…? She takes it to the nearest table and sets it down before removing the top. Peering inside she spies a unique and beautifully crafted skeleton key. She sticks two fingers into the small opening and pinches the key between the digits, removing it. Surveying it with the eye of an artist, she's impressed and wonders about who made it. Bringing her back to the question of how it came into her possession.

Oliver had been the only visitor to her workshop today and she highly doubts it came from the pragmatic man. Had her assistant left it for her? But, why would she put it in the lamp? Completely knackered from a long day, she doesn't feel as though she has the brain power to solve this puzzle. She slips the key in her pocket and resumes putting away the lamp. Then she locks up and takes a set of stairs in the back up to the apartment above. The area used to be additional office space and storage. After many, many nights of being here late and falling asleep on her couch, she finally renovated it into a living space. Eventually, she'd simply moved in, rather than using it as a place to crash.

When she reaches the top of the stairs, she takes her house key out of her back pocket and tries to unlock the door, but it won't twist. She wiggles it a little assuming it's sticking and then tries again, but it still won't engage the lock. Twisting around on the small landing, she leans her back against the wall and sags in exhaustion. This was not what she needed right now.

It had been a busy month as she tried to catch up on her work after taking a two week trip to Spain. She'd come home with a suitcase full of heartache to a chaotic schedule. Although, being busy could be seen as a silver lining since it left her almost no time to dwell on her broken heart. First thing, she needs to figure out is how to get inside her damn apartment.

The key she'd found in the lamp begins to hum with a low vibration, and when she pulls it out of her pants, it's also putting off a dim, effervescent glow. *Am I really that tired?* The thought to try it in her apartment door flits through her mind and at first, she dismisses it. But, when the idea gets more insistent, she tries is simply to get the feeling to stop nagging her. The little teeth on the end of the key slide right in and it twist easily, unlocking the door.

She backs up in surprise when she sees what is on the other side of the door and almost falls down the stairs. To counteract the gravity pulling her backwards, she lurches forward, stumbling past the door and flinches at the bang of the door as it slams shut. She tries the knob to open it back up and gives the door a dirty look when it doesn't budge. *Stupid twat.*

She turns, spinning in a slow circle, taking in her surroundings. The room looks like a big, open foyer, decorated in cream and gold, with a massive, crystal chandelier. Eyeing the tall, gold double doors, she figures the odds on being able to open it. With the way her life had been lately, her calculated guess is, her chances don't look good. The now familiar sound of the key draws her attention and she looks for it, finding it on the ground by where the other door . . . used to be? She freezes halfway to the floor and stares at the smooth, creaseless wallpaper; no door in sight. The key starts to practically bounce around like a Mexican jumping bean, breaking her out of her shocked state. Scooping it off of the travertine tile, she faces the set of doors again and approaches them, intent on trying the key in their lock, especially when she sees the engraving. That's what it's for, right? It works and she shrugs in acceptance. *Par for the weirdness course.*

An endless blue sky, full of twinkling stars, stretches out before her as she walks out onto a balcony. Along with the moon, they shed soft light on the scenery over the rail. The beauty draws her over to the barrier and she grips it with both hands, then gingerly leans out to get a good look at what's below her. It's perhaps twenty feet to the ground where a bright and colorful flower garden grows. Scanning the area, she determines that she has no clue where she is, not recognizing anything in the landscape.

Continuing her exploration, she spots a set of French doors made of lightly frosted, glass squares. They are open and white, filmy curtains billow out on the breeze, giving her a peek at the room beyond. Unsure whether she's trespassing, she creeps up to the doors, staying to the shadows. After several minutes, she doesn't detect any movement, so she tiptoes into what turns out to be a bedroom.

The décor makes her feel like she just entered an Arabian's princess's room. Lots of pillows and draping in brightly colored fabrics. A round canopy bed sits in the very center of the room with more hanging curtains and silky sheets. And, it's gloriously empty. Sabrina glances around again and comes to the conclusion that she is alone, so she pads over to the bed. She's about to climb up and collapse when she's startled by a rattling sound. Glancing around, she looks for the source and sees the lamp she'd created, sitting on a small, glass table. The sound is from the shaking clattering on the glass from spurts of shaking. Almost as if . . . The rest of this thought really hinges on whether or not she thinks she's dreaming. Because it seems as if something might be in there, trying to get out.

Oliver's joking description of the lamp comes back to her and she wanders over to it. She's about to lift the lid when she thinks better of it. Opening the lid of an unknown object that has something desperate to get out it. This never ends well in the movies. *Go to bed, Pandora.*

She's about to do as her inner voice suggests, then, at the last second, she spins around and snatches the lid off. Nothing happens. Well, crap. That was anticlimactic. With a disappointed sigh, she stares glumly at the golden lamp. Wait. She perks up as she remembers, you have to rub the lamp (or bottle if you're looking for Christina Aguilera) in order to release the—whatever. She grabs the lamp and rubs it swiftly between her hands, making a little wish, then steps back and watches it warily. The lamp begins to shake so hard it actually bounces on the table and she fleetingly hopes it doesn't shatter the glass. Abruptly, the lamp goes still and quiet. Confused, Sabrina glances all around, not really knowing what she is looking for. There had to be a reason for all of that. Everything looks the same, even the lamp is in the exact same spot as before. She huffs in annoyance and rolls her eyes before stomping over to the bed and pulling the covers back.

"Sabrina."

The covers drop from her hands and she spins around so fast she stumbles back into the bed. "Dominick?" she gasps. Her eyes dart around wildly, trying to figure out where he came from. But, more importantly, *what the fuck he is doing here*! Her heart is beating so hard, she can feel the crack expanding, especially with the cause standing in front of her.

"Did you just . . . but the lamp and . . . was that you inside?" She stumbles over her words, not only because she's flustered, but because she is very aware how ridiculous her question is.

"Are you asking if I'm the genie from your lamp, angel?" The endearment causes her stomach to flutter and her panties become damp.

"I—no, that is—" She stops and takes a breath. "Well, are you?"

"Maybe," he says mysteriously before he stalks forward and grasps her upper arms, lifting her to his eye level. His face is angry but the dark brown orbs are bright with heat. The way he used to stare at her before he would...

Dominick sucks her bottom lip into his mouth before covering her mouth with his and, like always, pushing all thoughts out of her head. He fills every nook and cranny of her mind with turbulent emotions; pain, lust, love, a cacophony of sound when mixed together with the pounding of her heart.

"I'm so fucking angry with you, angel," he growls against her lips in his sexy American accent. A few tears escape, sliding down her cheeks and he kisses each one away. "But, I've missed you even more."

His mouth crashes down over hers again and he groans, his

hands going everywhere at once, making her moan with need. She's missed him more than she ever thought she would. Eventually, he breaks the kiss and steps back, his eyes sweeping over her body with appreciation. Then the corners of his mouth tip down and his jaw hardens, as he scowls. "Please tell me you didn't wear this outside your bedroom," he grits out.

Unsure what he's referring to, she looks down. *Um, okay. This is interesting.* She hadn't noticed her state of dress, or lack of, depending on how you look at it. Clearly, it was the latter to Dominick. Her skirt is made of long, shimmery, gauzy material, and it's virtually see-through, displaying her white, barely-there panties. Her top is made of the same material and it hugs her upper body, stopping right above her belly button, and encasing her arms in long sleeves. Her breasts are almost spilling out of the white brazier underneath the transparent layer. Even though she's spinning out of control from the bombardment of emotions, she inwardly smiles. She looks good and she preens a little, knowing how Dominick is affected by her.

However, he's still glaring daggers at her, and she is quick to reassure him. "No, I haven't worn this outside." *As far as I know.*

"No one sees you like this but me, angel," he says, his voice a deadly calm. She nods and his expression softens minutely. "Good. Not only will you earn yourself a spanking, but I'd hate to have to kill someone for looking at my woman."

She skips right over the spanking part (for now) and focuses on the second. His woman? But what about what she'd done? She'd met Dominick at a museum on the second day of her vacation. He was tall, dark, and sexy. And, to top it off, he was also an artist. Painter. Desire had exploded between them and it was so strong and intense, they ended up fucking each other's brains out in his hotel room that night.

She'd thought it would be a one-night thing and even still,

she let—wanted him—to take her virginity. When he'd realized she was untouched, it seemed to ship him into a frenzy. He was still gentle with her, but it was like he couldn't get enough of her, he seemed crazed in his need and possession of her. In the morning, she'd attempted to make a graceful exit, but he got demanding and growly; sexy as hell. He'd taken her back to bed and kept her there all day.

More often than not, when she or her sisters travel, they use their mother's maiden name so they don't have to deal with the hoopla that comes with people knowing they are royalty. It was a chance for her to run away and escape the palace, figuratively speaking. So, she didn't think much of it. But, as they got to know each other, she truly enjoyed the way he made her feel "normal" and let the charade go on a little bit longer until it was the day before she was to go home and she still hadn't told him. One other thing she'd learned, he valued honesty, declaring he had no tolerance for liars.

She'd snuck out of his bed that night and cried the whole way home, as her heart slowly cracked further open with each mile that separated them. She didn't expect him to come after her when he read the note she'd left, explaining her lie but not actually divulging who she really was.

"I don't understand. I wasn't honest with you."

Dominick looks at her with censure, the way you would look at a naughty child. "And it won't happen again. Will it, Sabrina?"

She shook her head, justly chastised. "You still want to be with me?" she asks nervously, afraid to hope.

"Do you think me so shallow that I would tell you I love you and then simply let you run away from me without chasing your ass down?" A glimmer of vulnerability enters his eyes. "Do you love me, angel?"

"Of course!" she blurts, desperate to reassure him that he is everything to her. "I love you so much it tore me up inside when I left. But"—her eyes drop, her cheeks heating with embarrassment—"I assumed you wouldn't want me after you found I wasn't who I said I was."

"I'll admit, I was mad as hell and I'm still not happy about it. But what put me in a rage, what still fans my ire, is that you snuck out like a thief in the night. You simply left, rather than face what you'd done and, more importantly, without giving me the opportunity to decide for myself whether I still wanted to be with you."

"Um, exactly how mad *are* you?" she asks with wide, rounded eyes.

His head dips until his lips are at her ear. "Between the spanking and the fucking, don't expect to be able to walk or sit for a while." A shudder ripples through her and he groans, burying his head in her neck. He starts to kiss his way down but she stops him with a hand under his chin, encouraging him to look up and meet her gaze.

"You didn't answer my question earlier."

"Oh? What question was that, angel?" he purrs.

"Are you the genie from the magic lamp?"

He ponders for a moment, his eyes never leaving hers. "Let's say I am, what are your three wishes?"

Her cheeks heat and she considers whether she's brave enough to tell him. She is done lying to him, so she bolsters her courage and admits what she really wants. "I only have one wish." She takes a deep breath. "You."

"Done," Dominick says, the fire in his brown eyes burning hotter than ever.

"Really?" she asks, her voice raspy with some disbelief and a lot of soaring hope.

"I guess it doesn't matter if I'm the genie, after all." He smirks.

"Are you?" she asks, insisting on an answer.

Dominick laughs and gives her a short kiss. When he pulls

back, his eyes are a little more serious and his expression becomes earnest. "Sabrina, I will always do my best to give you anything you wish for."

"In that case, maybe I do want my other two wishes," she quips cheekily making him chuckle again. "I wish for you to take me to bed and I wish for you to ask me to marry you." She holds her breath as she waits for his answer. Had she been too bold, asked for too much too fast?

"Also done, and done. Like I said, angel—anything." He swept her into a tight embrace, sealing his mouth over hers. They both shudder at the contact, already anticipating what's coming (no pun intended).

Dominick lifts her onto the bed and she scoots to the middle, watching him as he shucks his linen pants and shirt. His erection is thick and hard, standing up against his stomach, and her mouth waters. "I think I should make things up to you," she says raggedly.

"Is that so?" His eyes twinkle with amusement, but they are still filled with hunger. "What have you got in mind, angel?"

"You, in my mouth." Saying it out loud has her body erupting with tingles.

"All right, angel. Whatever you wish. But, I want you naked first." He climbs up on the bed and straddles her legs before he starts to slowly remove her clothing. It doesn't last and in their impatience, they both end up tearing at the fabric to get it off as quick as possible.

Dominick scans her body up and down, open appreciation in his eyes. "You're gorgeous, angel." She blushes and it spreads down over her chest. "Hmmm," he hums. "I love to see you like this, naked, flushed with need. So damn fuckable."

Sabrina eagerly reaches for his long and full cock with one hand, attempting to wrap her fingers around the girth. It's too big, so she joins it with her other and pumps up and down his length twice, her thumb spreading the pre-come over the tip. He groans and her pussy is so wet, she feels some of it gliding down to the bed.

"I want to taste you, Dominick," she says as she leans up so she can slide her hands around him and grip his incredibly firm ass. He drops to his hands and knees, moving up so the tip of his cock rubs against her plump lips, making them shiny from the come leaking out. Her tongue darts out to taste him and she moans in delight.

"Take me in your mouth, angel," he commands. "Suck me."

Using her hands, she guides his thickness between her lips, then twists and pumps them as she takes deep him deep until he bumps the back of her throat and she gags.

"Fuck! It's the hottest thing in the world to see you gagging from taking my cock down your throat, angel." His hips buck when she hollows out her cheeks and takes a deep pull. "Oh, fuck yes! That's so amazing." His eyes had closed tight, his face a mask of concentration, but now, he looks down at her and she can see the barely restrained control. It's about to snap. "Are you ready, angel? I need to fuck your mouth, to come down your throat. You'll take it, angel. All of it." His voice is gruff from the effort it's taking him to hold back. He rises to his knees and reaches under her arms to pull her through his legs, sitting her up so her mouth is lined up with his groin.

She lets go of his cock long enough to whisper, "Yes, all of it." Then she licks around the head, takes him back in and hums.

"Yes!" he yells, right before he grabs on to the headboard and he begins to fuck her mouth, hard. His tempo keeps climbing until she is sucking in fast breaths through her nose, keeping her mouth full to the brim with his dick. "Suck it, angel. Hard. Just like that. Yes! Oh, fuck! Fuck! Fuck! Fuck!" he chants while his cock grows even bigger and harder until he suddenly grabs her behind the head and holds her still. He bucks one last time, going deep into the recesses of her mouth and erupting in an orgasm that fills her mouth, pouring down her throat. He roars her name as his body wracks with shudders, and she swallows seemingly never-ending jets of semen. Finally, he lets her go and slides his member from her mouth, grabbing her biceps and lifting her up from her knees, crashing his mouth down on hers. "Angel," he pants against her lips, "that was fucking amazing. Thank you."

She smiles. "You're welcome. But it wasn't completely selfless. Remember what I said about turnabout being fair play?"

Dominick throws his head back and laughs while she giggles. Then the funny ends and he returns her gesture by making her scream so loud, after four orgasms, she's lost her voice.

Dominick taps softly on the glass door of the jewelry store and waits, glancing around the picturesque town square where it's located. The area has been well preserved for decades; most of the buildings even look to be pre-war. He finds himself wishing he had his supplies with him; he'd love to do a series of paintings inspired by this charming scenery.

The sound of the lock disengaging brings him back to why he is here. A young blonde woman opens the door, smiling, and standing back for him to enter. "She's upstairs in her apartment," she says as she leads him to the back of the store, all the way to a set of stairs. She clasps her hands together and excitedly whispers, "Good luck." Then she's gone, making her way back to the front, getting everything ready to open for business in a couple of hours. He'd hoped to be here last night, but his plane had been delayed, so he called his informant, Sabrina's older sister Chloe, who put him in touch with the store clerk. He'd dreamt of his reunion with Sabrina the whole way, though he highly doubted it would be on the set of the next Aladdin movie.

It had only been through a stroke of luck that he even found Sabrina. Her country is on the smaller side and wasn't even on his radar, nor had it occurred to him that she was a princess. After searching for a few weeks, he'd relayed the story to his childhood friend, Damon, who had in turn, recognized the name and description. Pretty confident it was Sabrina St. Claire, he'd handed the phone over to the pop singer he guarded, and she confirmed it was her sister.

She'd been invaluable helping him to get everything in order before going to Sabrina. It also didn't hurt to hear she's been moping since she got home. He doesn't want his angel to be sad, but it gave him hope that she was as lost without him as he was without her.

He climbs the stairs to about halfway, then stops when he sees a figure huddled on the ground with her back against the wall, fast asleep. Jogging the rest of the way up, he reaches the landing and kneels by her side. "Sabrina." He keeps his voice low and soothing so he doesn't scare her. She mumbles something unintelligible in her sleep, and he chuckles at how cute she is. She's also the most gorgeous woman he's ever known, and despite her single act of dishonesty, he'd known she was genuine and kind. She was impossible not to love. He tries again, running a finger down her cheek as he speaks, "Wake up, angel."

"Dominick?" Her eyes flutter and she stares at him with disbelieving eyes. "What are you doing here? How did you find me?"

"You seriously underestimated my love for you, angel," he responds.

"Your love?" she squeaks with surprise. "Aren't you angry with me?"

He frowns. "I was furious with you, Sabrina, but you're mine, and my anger couldn't possibly dim my love for you. I'd rather move on to the good stuff, like taking you to bed." His eyes narrow, making his expression a little fiercer. "It won't happen again, will it, angel? Because I'm going to let it slide this time; I'm too fucking happy to have you in my arms. But, you can expect to get your ass spanked if it happens again."

Sabrina's face flushes red at his words and he raises an eyebrow. "Does the idea appeal to you, angel? Am I going to have to come up with a different punishment? One that doesn't get you hot and bothered?" He stops and thinks for a moment. "Never mind, I'm all for anything that gets you worked up and desperate to be fucked."

"Only if you realize turnabout is fair play," she jokes.

"Bring it, angel," he goads, laughing.

"I love you," she says suddenly and he stops laughing, but the joyous smile remains.

"How about I take you to bed, then you marry me, and then I'm yours and you're mine, forever?"

She looks at him strangely for a minute before murmuring, "Those would be my three wishes."

It's his turn to give an odd look, but he shrugs it off and kisses her passionately, then lingers over her lips for a moment. "Let's go inside, angel."

When she moves to stand, he beats her to it and helps her up. He glances around as if just remembering where they are. "Why are you out here?"

"My key wouldn't work in the lock last night, I must have sat down to figure things out and fell asleep."

He puts out his hand, palm up. "Let me try."

She rolls her eyes and snarks, "Because you have magical powers?"

He grins and wiggles his fingers until she passes over her house key. He slips it in the lock, pauses and says, "Open sesame." Then he rotates the key and the door swings open. "Looks like I've got the magic touch, after all."

Dear Cupid, arrows don't make you a man

~ ⚭ ~

OLIVER

I drop my head back and close my eyes in exasperation when I hear the bickering in the hallway outside my office. "Simon, Abbi, would you be so kind as to stop your squabbling and come in here?" I bellow.

The resulting extended silence almost has me laughing. Simon enters first, a dark scowl on his face, followed by a blushing and contrite Abbi. She sits demurely in a chair across from me while Simon flops down in his usual spot on my couch, glaring at the back of her head.

"What is it going to take for you two to get along?" I ask crossly. Neither of them answer, and I sigh. "Look, you're both excellent at your jobs and I'd hate to lose either one. But, you've got learn to work together civilly or shit won't get accomplished anyway, and I'll be transferring one of you to another office. Do I make myself clear?" I'm trying to remain stern, but Wilhelm is buzzing in my pocket, distracting me. *Abbi and Simon? Really?* They hate each other.

"Perfectly clear, Oliver. I apologize for being so unprofessional," Abbi replies. She quickly covers her mouth, smothering a yawn. Simon makes a noise that sounds something like an irritated grunt, causing Abbi to toss him a dirty look.

"Thank you, Abbi." I dismiss her and turn my laser focus on Simon, warning him not to push me too far. Once she's gone and has shut the door, I snap, "Get it together, Simon. You're acting like a child. And may I remind you, you are not irreplaceable. Although, it would be a massive pain in the ass to do so."

Simon folds his arms across his chest and glares at me. "Who is the jackass taking Abbi out every night? She comes in tired and dragging every day, barely staying awake at her desk. She's going to make herself sick. Then, where will we be?"

Wilhelm is still humming and it's for that reason alone, I give him some slack. Assuming his frustration stems from attraction and jealousy. "It's none of my business," I inform him, and because I'm a jackass, I needle him further. "It's none of your business, either, Simon. Unless she chooses to share it." The flare of conflicted emotions in his expression shouldn't amuse me, but it does. Must be the whole misery loves company shit.

I start thinking of ways to get the key to Abbi when Wilhelm goes silent. *No? Simon then?* He resumes his humming. My mind wanders back to Odette and how I'd simply given her the key. However, I decide that won't work for Simon since he'd be too stubborn to admit he wants to be her fantasy. *Idiot.* I can't wait for it to be Pippa's turn; I'm dying to know what she conjures up when she fantasizes about me. There is no doubt in my mind that she does.

Wilhelm is getting increasingly more obnoxious by the second and though I instinctively know I'm not supposed to tell Simon the purpose of the key. I am supposed to give it to him and it hits me then. "Simon, can you drop this on Abbi's desk on your way out?" I ask casually as I retrieve the key and toss it over to him.

He catches it and bows his head to examine it curiously. I start to count . . . 3 . . . 2 . . . 1. His head whips up. *There it is.* "Is this the skeleton key that was supposed to be in the box?" he asks incredulously. His eyes narrow suspiciously. "Why are you giving it to me? I don't want or need to deal with love. You've been enough proof of that."

"First, I'm not giving it to you, dipshit. I asked you to give it to Abbi." I watch to see if he understands the implication and almost smile when his eyes darken with anger. "And second, Pippa is worth anything and everything I've dealt with," I add because he needs a fucking wake-up call. "Even when she's being a pain in the ass, she is still the most perfect woman, because she was made to be mine." I cringe inside because, while this is true, I'm tempted to check and see if I've grown vagina from all of this mushy bullshit. I really don't understand why Cupid is portrayed as a man. The arrows don't make up for the fact that he is a pussy.

Simon scowls to cover up the hint of yearning creeping into his eyes. "Not interested," he lies. "But, I'm happy for you."

"Simon," I start, shaking my head with fake sympathy, "I've come to the conclusion that you are either living in denial or just completely stupid." He's shooting daggers at me and I fight a smile, returning his expression mockingly. "Now, get the fuck out of my office. I've got work to do. And, I suggest you man up, and go after your girl."

When I get home in the evening, I find my way into the room next to my office to check the progress. I went ahead with my plans to build a workspace for Pippa, right next to mine, with a shared door, of course. I've decided to work from home more often so I can spend more time with my family, and I want her near. The thought of a midday fuck on my desk may have spurred me into action, but I would have done this eventually. The room is almost done, mint green painted walls, hardwood floors, walls of bookshelves and white, distressed furniture. Staring at her desk, where she will write steam and romance, and the aforementioned, midday fucking session, have put me in a painful spot. *At least you know you've still got a cock down there instead of a shiny new vagina.*

When I get into my empty bed at night, I vow the next two nights are the last I spend without Pippa. With all of her sisters taken care of, we'll spend tomorrow night in her fantasy, and I'll give her one day to get ready for her wedding. By the third night, she'll be permanently installed in my bed, and I won't let her out until she's pregnant. Maybe not even then.

Meanwhile...

Abbi's Fantasy (and sometimes Simon's)

∽◦∾

NO MORE RUINED SHOES

"Here." Something heavy punks down and slides across Abbi's desk, obviously having been tossed there unceremoniously. She sighs and looks up at the blond-haired, blue-eyed, extremely well-built, Adonis, who seems intent on making her life a living hell. He has a look of complete loathing on his face and if his eyes weren't glued to the object, she might have thought it was directed at her. He points at the object. "Oliver asked me to deliver this to you."

She gazes down and sees a skeleton key made of gold. It's rather odd. She's never seen anything like it before. "What is it for?"

"Well, it's a key, Princess," he explains as though talking to a child. "It unlocks . . . things."

Abbi gasps and widens her eyes in pretend shock. "Thank heavens you were here, Simon! I might have tried to eat it! Seeing as how I'm teething and all," she finishes dryly. He opens his mouth to say something that will no doubt make her want to throat punch him, but he doesn't get the chance.

"Both of you! Take the rest of the day off before I fire you!" Oliver shouts from inside his office.

They glare accusingly at each other and Abbi asks quietly, "What am I supposed to do with this . . . what did you call it? Key?"

Simon doesn't respond right away and for a half of a second, she thinks there is a glimmer of humor in his eyes. She'd seen the same flash before, during some of their many, many arguments. And, just like all of those other times, she wonders if she's seen it at all.

"Nothing, Princess. It does nothing. I suggest you put it in a drawer and hang on to it until Oliver comes to his senses and wants it back." She hates when he calls her that, but she doesn't tell him because he'd probably call her by it more often, just to piss her off. Before he turned into the big bad wolf, he used to call her "love." She'd melted every time.

"Sure, I'll do that," she deadpans and drops the key into her purse, ignoring his glower. She had a very restless sleep last night and she doubted tonight would be any better, but she couldn't bring herself to truly care. Her nights are the time when she is happiest, then morning comes and Simon ruins it. Maybe tonight would be one of those nights where she'd be forced to call in sick tomorrow.

Simon watches her ass and hips sway as she gets into the elevator, then storms to his office, slamming the door behind him. He's tempted to start throwing things, but he knows it won't relieve all of his pent up aggression from... He sighs. Oliver is right. He needs to stop living in denial. The truth is, its sexual frustration. It has him tied in knots and it's only getting worse.

He's wanted Abbi since the day he met her, and as they worked together, he felt like they were growing closer. They'd even gone to lunch together regularly, and he made the decision to ask her out but hadn't had the chance. Then, a few weeks ago, she started to come in exhausted and was calling in sick more than usual. He'd thought maybe it had to do with Oliver's seemingly permanent transformation into an ogre. But, there were times he would catch her sitting at her desk with a dreamy look on her face, often with a small smile, and humming. It always seemed to happen when she was the most exhausted.

He finally went to her desk, sat on the edge and offhandedly asked what she'd done the night before. She'd blushed and said, "We were at—" He bristled at the plural term and shot to his feet, interrupting what she was going to say.

"I'm glad you had so much fun you exhausted yourself, but maybe you should contain it to the weekend. You're not good to us here if you are too tired to do your job."

Her jaw dropped to the ground and she'd snapped, "Has my productivity gone down?"

"Not yet," he hissed before turning away and shutting himself in his office. He'd been consumed with jealousy but somehow convinced himself it was self-righteous anger at her trivial attitude towards her job. He started to use every excuse possible to argue with her, knowing in those moments she was only thinking about him. And, he enjoyed seeing her all fired up, though he pays for those instances when he has to talk down a raging hard on.

It's time for this to end. Simon grabs his keys and stalks to his office door. He didn't really believe in the power of the skeleton key. It had mostly been a way to give Oliver something else to try while he came up with more options. But, no matter what this key thought, Abbi was his. He decides to follow her, to see this guy he was going up against and, just in case, make sure she doesn't try to use the key.

≈

After coming home, Abbi spends the afternoon and evening puttering around the castle. As it nears bedtime, her anticipation grows and at half an hour to midnight, she hurries to get ready for bed. She hops in and snuggles down into the covers, daydreaming about Simon, and waiting for sleep to take her.

12:10: Awake.

12:20: Still awake.

12:30: Seriously?

12:40: What the hell is that buzzing noise?

Irritated beyond belief, she throws the covers off and climbs out of bed, listening intently to find out where the humming is coming from. Following the sound, she ends up at her purse which it hanging in her closet. She digs through for the culprit and finds it is the skeleton key Simon had given her earlier. It has a sort of golden glow now and it's vibrating. Weird. She turns it all around, looking to see if there is an on/off button that got pushed by accident, but she doesn't find anything. It's all smooth glass.

Still holding onto it, she wanders out of the closet and, much to her disappointment, giving up on sleep, she drifts down to the kitchen for a snack. If she can't figure out how to shut it off, she'd leave it in the living room under a pillow or something until morning.

Entering the kitchen, she stops in her tracks when she sees a light, eerily similar to the one coming from the key, peeking out from under the door to her storage closet. Approaching it slowly, she notices the key's vibration increases, pulsing wildly in her hand. When she gets to it, she stands there, every scary movie scenario running through her mind. Freaking her out even more is that some invisible force is making her hand feel like it *needs* to unlock the door. She considers waking Pippa so she doesn't have to investigate this on her own. Then, she thinks about how crazy she'll look if they get back down to the kitchen and there is nothing there. So, she throws her shoulders back boldly, trying to convince herself she can do this alone.

I ain't afraid of no ghosts. She giggles and it bolsters her bravado a notch. Trying the knob first, she's not surprised to find it locked. It seems to fit correctly into the storyline of whatever horror movie she's starring in. Perhaps it's *The Skeleton Key* and this is where she's going to have her soul sucked out and put into the body of some old woman who is about to die. *That would really suck.*

Abbi rolls her eyes at herself; she's an adult, not twelve. This is real life, not a movie. And, she needs to stop procrastinating. Using the skeleton key, she unlocks the door and holds her breath (in fear or courage, she isn't really sure which) and pulls it open.

It's definitely nothing like she expected. The foyer is gorgeous; the kind of room she would expect to see before she entered the pearly gates of heaven. Except, there are large golden doors instead. She walks to the doors, figuring she's come this far, she might as well complete the journey. The lock has an etching above it and it looks exactly like the key in her hand, further confirming her decision to keep going. Using the key once more, she's able to push open one of the heavy doors and what she sees puts a big smile on her face. She must have fallen asleep after all because she steps into the place where her dreams always begin.

Simon throws his hand in front of the door, catching it before it closes, determined to go after Abbi. He had come to the palace this afternoon under the guise of needing to use the library for "research" again. He kept an ear out for the doorbell so he would know when Abbi's date came to pick her up. When it hit ten o'clock and she hadn't left, he breathed a sigh of relief, thinking her evening was probably cancelled. At midnight, the queen stopped into the library and invited him to stay overnight. He gratefully accepted and let her mother him, making sure he'd eaten and which room he'd like, what did he want for breakfast? He had no doubt Abbi would be like that one day, selflessly caring for everyone, and gaining great joy from it.

It made him love her more. *What the actual fuck?!* He loved her? He fucking *loved* her? Yeah, okay. He was head over fucking heels. Remembering Oliver's second suggestion, to man up and go after his girl, he figured admitting he loved her was a good start.

After the queen got him settled in a guest chamber, he'd snuck up to the wing where Abbi's room was and found an empty room, right next door. He wasn't even really sure what he was waiting for, but when she came out and headed down the hallway, he followed. *Stalker much?* This isn't the same thing . . . he doubted the royal guards would agree. Not that it would stop him.

He pokes his head around the corner, peering inside just in time to see Abbi disappear through a set of massive golden doors. Stepping all of the way inside, his mouth opens, and he turns in an awed circle. Has this always been here? He knows it's a stupid question, but the possibility that it has makes him feel better, like there isn't something magical going on. Then he spots the skeleton key she left in the lock of one of the golden doors. Shit. What if she's in there with her true love? He didn't want to see it, but he knows he's going to look. He can't not look.

He turns the key and grasps the large handle, slowly dragging it open, and finding himself in another jaw-dropping moment. He's at the top of long staircase and, to his left, there is a royal guard, slumped in a chair with a cup in his hands, and fast asleep. Curiously, Simon grabs the cup and sniffs it, smelling wine and something else, but he's not sure what it is. He has a hunch it's what put the man into a slumber.

Remembering his purpose, he turns back to the stairs and begins to descend them as stealthily as possible. He spots Abbi at the bottom, relieved to see she is no longer wearing the silky little pajama set she had on. When she left her room earlier, he almost dragged her back inside to see what she looks like underneath it. Then, when she went through the doors, he could feel anger building at others seeing her dressed like that. He didn't have time to give in to it, though, staying focused, eyes on the prize. Now, he can put it out of his mind because, by the glimpse he got, she is now wearing a formal dress. Glancing down at his t-shirt and pajama pants, he shrugs and continues on.

At the bottom, he finds himself on a path that leads through a grove of trees, all blooming with silver leaves. Real silver? He touches one and it breaks off, falling into his palm, and it is, indeed, real. Putting the leaf in his pocket, he journeys along the path until he enters a second grove. This time, the leaves appear to be made of gold and just like with the silver, he takes one and discovers it's the genuine thing. It joins the silver and he starts moving again.

He's not able to see Abbi anymore, but her footsteps are clear in the dirty path he's walking, so he knows he is going in the right direction. The path veers left, and he's astonished to find himself in a third grove. The trees are glittering with— holy shit—they are fucking diamonds! He grabs one and it shimmers in his palm. *This is unreal.* An inner voice replies with a sarcastic, "Yes. Yes, it is unreal." *Point taken.* He slips the diamond in with the gold and silver. Once he's paying attention to his course again, he sees that the path ends soon.

At the mouth of the grove, it opens to a great, clear lake. Abbi is just stepping into one of twelve empty boats that resemble a gondola. He calls out to her, but a gust of wind carries his voice in the opposite direction and he starts to run towards her. Before he can reach her, the boat has pushed off, and the gondolier is steadily taking it to the other side, where he can vaguely make out the outline of a castle.

"I need you to take me over there," Simon demands one of the other gondoliers.

The man shakes his head, "I'm sorry, signore. I have to wait for the other princesses."

Other princesses? Simon looks around at the eleven empty boats then back to the man. "Do all twelve of them come every night?"

He shakes his head, his eyes a little sad, "No, signore. They all used to come frequently, but it's only been Princesses Abbi for some time now. But, we need to be here in case another one does wish to go across the lake."

Simon scrubs his hands down his face, tired and frustrated. "Look, Giovanni—"

"My name is Bartolomeo, signore," he interrupts, obviously confused.

Simon sighs, "Ok. Look, Bart, the other princesses are each with the love of their life, they won't be coming anymore, I'm sure of it. And, even if they did, those sweet sisters would wait for you to return." His manipulations tactic works and Bart nods.

"Yes, the princesses would never be upset. Go ahead, signore, get in. I will take you across the lake." Relieved, Simon hops into the boat and Bart pushes off. They are moving at a slow and steady pace, forcing Simon to bite his lip so he won't shout at the guy to go faster.

Abbi grins as her sweet, old friend, Piero, brings the gondola to a stop by a dock and secures it. He helps her to step from the boat, then hands her a brand new pair of shoes. "To replace the ones you wore out last night, Princess," he sings with an answering smile.

She laughs and gratefully takes the proffered slippers. "As with every time; thank you, Piero." She waves as she prances up the path to the castle. When she arrives at the vast entrance, she looks up and is surprised to see her own home. Usually, she dreams of different unique castles. She smiles at the thought of being with her suitor in her palace; it would feel more real than ever before.

She picks up the front of her delicate, gold gown and excitedly enters the castle, stopping at the entrance to their grandest ballroom. It's been decorated lavishly, lit with crystal chandeliers, and blazing torches flanking every set of doors to the veranda that wraps around two sides of the room. Scanning the crowd, she looks for him, running over every face in detail until her heart drops into her stomach and tears prick her eyes. He isn't here.

More sedately now, she makes her way down the steps into the stunning ballroom and weaves through the crowd to get to the refreshment table. Taking some cookies on a little china plate and a glass of lemonade, she roams out to the veranda and takes a seat on an outdoor swing. She nibbles on her treats, her feet pushing off the ground, gently rocking her. This is certainly an odd night. What's the point of coming to the ball if you can't wear out your shoes dancing with the man you love?

"Abbi? Love?"

At the sound of Simon's voice, her heart soars and she stands quickly, her plate and cup crashing to the floor. She doesn't even notice the mess as she runs at Simon and launches herself into his arms. "I didn't think you were coming!" she exclaims, burying her face in the space between his neck and shoulder. Simon always smells amazing, like the forest, a woodsy scent that never fails to make her panties wet when it's coming from him.

"How did you know I'd be here, Abbi?" His voice is full of confusion and she looks up with a frown.

"You're always here. This is our time, you and me, when the world outside doesn't exist, and, you don't hate me."

His face softens and he gently kisses her lips. "Abbi, I never hate you. I'm always hopelessly in love with you," he insists.

"Right," she agrees. "Here. We are always in love here." She abstains from reminding him how he treats her in their everyday reality. It should never intrude on their fantasy.

Simon sighs. "Let's pretend this is our first night meeting at a ball like this. Show me how our night would go."

She laughs and looks at him like he's crazy, then shrugs. Why not? "Well, first, we dance. And, you hold me in your arms as though you'll never let me go."

He gathers her up close to him and starts to sway to the music floating through the open veranda doors. "Like this?" His voice is husky and sensual. Warmth infuses her and she shivers from the cool night air on her suddenly, overheated skin.

"Mm hmm," she answers, putting her arms around his neck and clinging to him, afraid to let go. What if her bubble bursts and he disappears? She shakes the thought away and focuses on the peace of being in his arms. The feeling of being completely and utterly loved.

"You look incredibly beautiful tonight, my love," he says softly.

"You're not so bad yourself," she retorts with a wink. With a puzzled frown, he looks down. His eyebrows shoot up at the sight of his very dapper tuxedo, as though he was expecting to be wearing something else. But, then he smiles at her and all of her thoughts are wiped away, mesmerized and so very in love with him.

They dance for hours, every song acting like an aphrodisiac, each one stronger than the last. His erection has been pressing against her all night, her nipples are tight, her every movement causing her dress to abrade them and she knows by the end of the evening, her panties are completely ruined. Finally, Simon has enough. He picks her up and cradles in his arms as he carries her to the hallway outside the ballroom. She giggles at his determined walk, knowing exactly where they are going and why. He seems to get a little turned around at one point and she whispers directions in his ear.

Reaching her room, he stalks inside and kicks the door shut. He spins around and sets her down only to grab her ass and hoist her up so her legs immediately wrap around his waist. He crashes his mouth down over hers and walks forward two steps until her back is against the door. The thick bulge in his pants is pressing her into the wall, the heat of his cock warming her pussy, even through all the layers of clothing. "Simon. Please..." she mumbles.

He tears his mouth from hers and his blue eyes, filled to the brim with need, stare deeply into her green ones. "What, love. What can I do for you?" His tone is almost pleading, begging her to tell him how to please her. Flames seem to be licking her everywhere, stinging her skin, and sending sparks of lust straight to her pussy. He shifts and she cries out at the sensation as his cock rubs against just the right spot.

"Do you want me to make love to you?" he asks brokenly, his panting making it hard to talk.

"Can you—um..." Abbi pauses, blushing to the roots of her hair and looking anywhere but at him. She clears her throat and tries again. "You always make love to me and it's amazing, earth-shattering, but I was wondering if maybe this time you could um—" She stops again, about to give up on finding the courage to ask for what she wants.

"Are you asking me to fuck you, love?" He chokes on the

question, and she brings her gaze back to his face, wondering if he's embarrassed too. But, what she sees is stark need, desperation, and ravenous hunger. All for her.

"Yes. I want you to . . . do that."

A glimmer of playfulness appears and he smirks at her. "Do what, love?"

"Um, what you said before," she hedges.

"You want me to fuck you?"

"Yes, er, that."

"You have to say it, love," he taunts.

"I want you to"—her eyes close and her voice drops to a whisper,—"*fuck me.*" She swallows hard, trying not be embarrassed and looks up at Simon through her lashes. The humor is gone and all that's left is raw want.

"Hot as fucking hell, Abbi," he croaks before kissing her hard, his tongue plunging into her mouth, tangling with hers. He removes one hand from her butt cheek and scrunches up the fabric of her skirt until he can glide it over the smooth skin of her thigh, and return to her ass. Where he encounters more naked flesh. "Damn it, are you wearing a thong?" She nods, so lost in him she's unable to form words. His hands clench and he rocks into her. Just like that, she cries out and goes off like a rocket, bursting with streams of sparkles that rain down around her.

Simon curses and fumbles to get his other hand under her skirt and palming the other side of her ass. His lips glide over her neck, sucking at her pulse point, feeling the rapid beat of her heart as she comes back down to earth. He drags his hand over her skin until he's at her pussy, then slips a finger under the drenched fabric. "Abbi, oh, damn. You are soaked, so ready for me." With a twist of his fingers and a flick of his wrist, he tears her panties away.

"You wanted me to fuck you, love, and after seeing you come, feeling how wet you are for me, I don't think I can do anything else. You are so gorgeous, Abbi, but watching you like that, knowing I'm the reason for the ecstasy . . . I need you. *Now*."

Abbi's legs are tight around his hips, her body still shuddering with aftershocks, but his words have her core clenching, and he grunts at the contact when her legs spasm around him, pulling him impossibly closer. Using his lower body to hold her up, he grips the fabric of her dress and tears it down the center. Again, he clasps her ass and stares at her bare breasts, then drops his head back with closed eyes, breathing deeply.

Bringing his head back up, he moves his groin back a little, and she whimpers. "Take me out, love," he commands softly. Her eyes flutter as she processes his words, a greedy smile forming on her face. She'd always been too shy with Simon, even in these dreams, to ask for this. Now she was going to have her world rocked, hard and fast. Taking her arms from around his neck, she unzips his pants and reaches inside to grip his considerable girth. She gasps, not remembering it being quite this big. Will he even fit? Simon seems to sense her turmoil and he nibbles on her ear. "Your pussy is the exact right size for my cock, love. Because I exist only for you. Trust me, we fit."

It's a good thing he's holding her up, because she practically melts. Looking down at the tip, sticking just above the low waistband of his pants, she frowns at how red and angry it looks. "Are you in pain?" She runs the pad of her thumb over the tip, spreading around the liquid escaping the slit.

"Yeah, love. I'm in pain, and I will be until I'm buried deep inside your pussy."

Gingerly, she gets him all the way out and pushes his pants so they fall to the ground. Commando? Wow, he'd never done that in any of her fantasies before. Her eyes meet his and they stay locked on each other as he lines up with her pussy and pushes inside. She gasps at the fullness and the way he's stretching her. This is all a little overwhelming and confusing. She's never experienced this kind of pain, or the satisfying feeling of being filled by her man. He pulls back an inch and pushes in again, going a little further until he bumps her barrier.

Ok, that was definitely not there in her dreams before.

"Fuck. You're a virgin, Abbi?" he grits, clearly struggling not to move. She flushes with embarrassment. "Hey, hey, now," he says quickly. "There is nothing in this world, other than your love and our children, that is a more precious gift than choosing me as your first."

"Really?" She perks up at his beautiful words.

"Really," he repeats. "As long as you understand, not only am I the first, I am your *only*. You are mine, Abbi St. Claire. Oh, about that, we'll discuss your change in name later. After I've had my way with you. Multiple times." He shifts and moans, a low, guttural sound. "You being a virgin, just means I can't fuck you like I wanted to."

"Yes, you can," she disagrees.

"No, love. This is going to hurt. I need to be gentle."

"But, I don't want—" He stops her by sealing his mouth over hers and he begins to move again, pulling out just a little and he stops, getting ready to break the thin membrane. Not one to give up so easily, Abbi grabs his ass and squeezes with all her might as she bites down on his lip. The move takes him completely off guard and between the shock and the roaring lust streaming through his body, he loses his tightly reined control and thrusts in hard, driving all the way in, bumping her cervix. She cries out from the pain but refuses to give him time to come to his senses.

She stiffens her legs and tenses the muscles of her pussy, then bucks her hips and she digs her fingers into his ass cheeks. "*Fuuuuuck!*" he roars. In this split second, he becomes more animal than man. He pounds into her relentlessly, and she screams with each deep plunge. Her back slams into the door a couple of times before the noise seems to make its way to his ears. He growls and holds her against him, keeping their connection as he stalks over to the bed. He climbs up and takes her legs from around him, pulling all the way out. She makes a sound of protest that turns into a yelp of pain when his hand comes down on her naked ass.

He flips her around and onto her knees, then guides her hands to the headboard, wrapping her fingers around it. "You wanted me to lose control, love? Well, I did," he growls almost angrily. "I'm going to fuck you like the animal you've unleashed and you're going to take what I give you."

Apparently, she doesn't answer fast enough because her ass stings from another hard slap. "Hold on tight, love," he warns. Gripping her hips, he slams back inside of her, picking up speed with each thrust. His hands travel around to her front and he palms her breasts, squeezing them, then pinching the nipple hard enough to make them throb in a mixture of pleasure and pain. She whimpers and he removes one hand to spank her ass on each of his next three thrusts, then switches hands, giving her other her breast and ass cheek the same treatment.

"Fuck yes, take it, Abbi. Damn you feel good, so fucking tight. Let me hear you." He spanks her again and she whimpers. "Louder, Abbi," he demands. She finally let's go of any lingering inhibitions and just feels. Feels the way his cock drags against the walls of her pussy, the way it stretches her to what feels like a breaking point. She revels in the building pressure, the sting of his spanks and twists of her nipples, and the resulting pleasure that floods her body and coats his cock in her arousal. "That's it, love," he encourages, and she suddenly realizes she is screaming with every movement, his name flying from her lips.

"Yes! Yes! Simon, oooooh, yes!"

"If you could see this view," he moans. "Fuck. Your sweet red ass, my cock disappearing inside your hot pussy and coming out covered in your cream."

His filthy mouth builds her up, putting every nerve on alert, her muscles all clenched in anticipation. He abruptly stills his hips and grabs her breasts, bringing her up on her knees, her back against his chest. "I need you to come, love," he says right before he slaps her pussy and she shatters like a window, each crack building and building until finally, she explodes into a million tiny shards of glass.

As she comes, he puts a hand on her back and gently pushes her back down, all the way to the bed, so her shoulders are on the mattress with her ass high in the air. He wraps his arms around her legs and applies pressure, guiding them open as wide as they will go. "Tilt your pussy, love." She angles is as best she can in this position. He bends over and plays with her nipples, his hips still, so she can feel every beat of his heart through the pulse of his cock.

She moans, "No, Simon, I can't take anymore." Then gasps from the pain of his hand landing on the raw skin of her ass. Her pussy floods with juices and they run down her legs.

"What did I tell you when you made me lose control, Abbi?" he snaps.

"I—I would, ooooh, I had to take it," she concedes, her voice hoarse and low.

"That's right. And, I want you to come again. We're going to go together this time, so don't come unless I tell you."

"Oo—okay."

"Good girl," he purrs. He plays with her nipples some more, lazily beginning to thrust his cock in and out. Then he slides his hands down to her pussy, spreading the lips and as his hips pump faster, he drives her crazy with touches around her clit, passing over it only enough to tease.

"Simon, please!" she begs. He slams into her again, over and over, and she feels herself about to fall over the edge when he pinches one of her nipple hard enough for the zing on pain to penetrate her fog.

"Not yet," he snaps, then resumes his erratic thrusting and pussy play. "Almost, love. Oh, shit, shit, fuck! *Almost*—fuck! NOW!" he bellows, pinching her clit hard and planting himself deep inside her they are connected with no air or space between them. Making them one. "Fuck yes, Abbi, yes!" His come is filling her with its heat. His lazily pushes in and out of her as they ride out their orgasms. Then they collapse on the bed in a sweaty, sated heap of tangled limbs.

An hour or so later, they lay in bed, Simon on his back, slowly running his fingers through her hair as she rests her head on his chest. She yawns and blinks her eyes rapidly, trying to rid them of their sleepy heaviness. "Why don't go to sleep, love?" Simon suggests.

Her face rubs against his smattering of chest hair when she shakes her head, then yawns again. "I don't want the night to be over. I hate when morning comes and we are enemies again." Her voice is forlorn, and Simon adjusts her so she is now sprawled on top of him, her chin propped on her folded hands.

"It won't happen, love. I could never forget what happened tonight. Now that I've admitted to you and to myself, how desperately in love with you I am, I can't shove it back into the box. It won't fit and it's growing by the minute."

She smiles and looks at him strangely. "You tell me you love me every time we meet in my dreams; why do you seem so surprised?"

Simon shrugs. "I don't know," he says cagily. "Perhaps it seems more real tonight than it has before." He palms her ass and tugs her so she's straddling him right over his rapidly growing erection. He gives her a naughty smile and a wink. "If you need something to wake you up, I have a few suggestions."

~

Simon groans at the sunlight streaming onto his face. He doesn't want to wake up and go back to reality. Last night, he'd had the best dream and it had opened his mind so he couldn't hide anymore. Now, the hard part would be convincing Abbi to forgive him, and he'd loved her all along, but was fighting it, turning him into a monumental asshole. What he wouldn't give to go back into his fantasy where he fell asleep holding her luscious body close. He mentally grins. After fucking her four times, of course.

Something warm and soft shifts over his body. What the hell? He pries an eye open and freezes. This isn't his room. He glances down and holds his breath, afraid to do anything that might break him out of what is obviously a hallucination. Was he still dreaming?

Abbi is sleeping on top of him, her cheek pressed to his chest, her mouth slightly open so he can feel her hot breath on his skin. Her plump breasts are pillowed against him, and her arms are banded around his waist, holding tightly as though she fears he'll get away. She shifts again and he groans when her pussy rubs against his morning wood. It's slick with her juices. She's wet for him, even in her sleep, and he fights the need to rock his hips up. Damn, he wants her.

Suddenly, her muscles tense and her head slowly rises, turning to face him, her eyes bleary and confused. "Simon?" She stares at him warily, before dropping her gaze and gasping as she realizes she's lying on top of him, butt naked. She squirms and Simon grabs her waist to still her movement even as he moans.

"Don't move like that, love, or you're going to find yourself impaled on my cock for a morning fucking."

Her eyes widen and she shakes her head as though she thinks it will change what she is currently seeing and feeling. "Am I still dreaming?" she whispers.

He brushes some of her hair away from her face, tucking it behind her ear. "I wondered too, but, either way, we're together and." He swallows the lump forming in his throat, wishing away the vulnerability. "We love each other, right?"

Abbi searches his eyes with deep intensity, looking for something. He doesn't shutter his emotions, deciding to lay it all out for her. After a minute, a beautiful smile graces her face, lighting up his world. "You love me?"

"Desperately," he breathes.

"I love you, too."

Grasping her chin, he captures her lips for a deep kiss, both of them giving each other a part of their souls. Then he tears his mouth from hers and says firmly, "You're going to marry me."

"Are you asking?" She raises an eyebrow reprovingly.

There is not one second of hesitation before he answers, "No. It's a fact. We're getting married and we're going to make lots of little Abbies." He grins at her indignant look, and she isn't able to keep it up, melting into a dreamy smile.

"Okay. You've got yourself a deal."

And then there were none. Except me

PIPPA

There are moments in your life you just can't unsee, all you can do it pray to never experience them in the first place. Seeing my sister kissing a guy (Simon? Interesting)? Not really at that level. Seeing my sister virtually mauling the guy who is clearly sneaking out after having spent the night? I could have gone my whole life without seeing *that*. I sink into a chair at the kitchen table and plunk my elbows down with my hands over my eyes. I hear some whispering and some more heavy silence, a little more whispering, and hallelujah, the door clicks shut.

"Oh," Abbi says in surprise. "Hey, Pippa."

"Is it safe to uncover my eyes?"

Abbi snorts. "We weren't that bad."

I uncover my eyes warily and when I see Simon isn't here, I put my hands down. "Abs, you were practically making babies right there in the doorway."

Abbi laughs and strolls towards the back staircase. "No, that's what we were doing in my bedroom last night and this morning."

I slap my hands over my ears. "No, no, no. Just—*no*," I

groan. She rolls her eyes and bounces up the stairs. I sigh and stand up, then wander around the kitchen looking for something to eat. I'm too nervous to put anything in my stomach, so I give up and go back to my room. My time is up, it's been eleven days since I laid down the gauntlet and, in this short span, all eleven of my sisters have gotten engaged. Abbi and Simon may not have announced yet, but let's be real— even if they are already making babies—he better put a ring on it soon, or I'm going to kick his ass. Or, make Oliver do it for me since I'm less than half Simon's size.

Anyway, back on topic. I agreed to marry Oliver after all of my sisters were either engaged or married. Oh, did I forget to mention, three of them eloped in the last two days? Pardon my oversight. It could be a coincidence, but it would be an awfully big one. I can't help the niggling feeling Oliver has had something to do with it. I'm starting to wonder if Oliver is some kind of wizard/Cupid—let's hope he's wearing briefs instead of a diaper. *Or better yet, commando.* I even had the strangest dream about Oliver and a really cool looking skeleton key. In the dream, he slipped it to each of my sisters to help them and their loves find each other. Weird, right?

With everyone paired off, I'm the only one left. But, the truth is, I stopped denying my love for Oliver a few days ago. As well as the fact that I really do want to be his wife, to have his children, and to make a home with him. It's not a fear of living up to my end of the bargain that has my stomach in knots. It's the fear that he may have changed his mind.

Private Wilhelm is AWOL

OLIVER

My turn. My eyes pop open and I sit up in bed, wide awake. Day twelve. *At last, it's my turn.* I throw the covers off, get out of bed, and march over to Wilhelm's box. *All right, buddy, I'm the last man standing.* Opening the lid—"What the fuck?!"

It's empty. The damn fucking box is *empty*! I shake my head in disbelief. This isn't happening. *Let's try this again.* I slam the lid down and count to one hundred. Why? It seemed like the thing to do, now pipe down. With a deep inhale, I open it again and . . . it's still unoccupied. Its previous tenant probably having a good laugh at my rapidly building panic. Pippa's sisters have all found love, and while this means Pippa needs to live up to her end of the bargain, I was counting on her fantasy tonight to help her admit how much she really wants the life we are going to have together. I wanted her to enter our marriage willingly, happily. *Go figure.*

I almost toss the box at the wall. Almost. Part of me is hoping this is Wilhelm's idea of a joke and he will show up later. It seems like something the little bastard would do. I back away slowly, ready to catch him in the act, but after an indeterminable amount of time, I give up. I've a lot of shit to do today. I'll worry about him later.

After I'm ready for the day, I set up the house for my evening plans with Pippa. It doesn't take long and I find myself restless, so I check on the AWOL Wilhelm, and when I don't find him, I decide to head into work. I had taken the day off but now, hopefully, it will get my mind off of things. I certainly don't need to be sitting around thinking of all the creative ways I'm going to make love to my Pippa tomorrow night. Knowing I won't be able to do anything if I can't check on Wilhelm, I grab the box and take it with me.

Abbi is sitting at her desk when I arrive and she greets me with a beaming smile. It appears Simon and Abbi found their way to each other last night. So, where the fuck is Wilhelm? I put on a front for her and greet her as happily as possible, then storm into my office and slam the door shut, effectively ruining my efforts.

I manage to get a little work done, but it's like pulling teeth. I can only imagine this is what Pippa feels like when she has writer's block. At one point in the day, a very jolly Simon and a blushing Abbi, pop in to tell me they are engaged. They were worried about being able to work together in the office now that they are a couple. I don't have a problem with it as long as they keep their sexcapades out of the office. Considering the day dreams I have about bending Pippa over this desk, I should probably feel like a hypocrite. *Fuck that. I own the place.*

The conversation only serves to remind me of Wilhelm, who I've officially labeled a deserter. I tamp down the urge to bang my head against my desk and decide it's time to move my plans along. I made them; I don't have to stick with my intended timetable. Wilhelm has blown them all to hell anyway.

I head home and up to my bedroom to change, setting the

empty box back on the dresser before going into the closet. My tux is hanging, freshly pressed, ready to put on, but when I reach for it, it feels wrong. I have a night of romance planned, with a gourmet dinner, crystal, champagne, and looking irresistible in Armani.

A memory forms in my mind, a random moment when Pippa had offhandedly mentioned how hot she thinks I look in jeans and a t-shirt. She rarely wears anything fancier than a summery type of skirt and pretty top, unless they are going to a function that calls for it. It's one of the things I love about her—she's laid back, doesn't put on airs, and is sassy as hell. It hits me; I've been going about this all wrong.

Pippa — O, Oliver — I lost count...

I fidget on the black leather seat of the car Oliver sent to pick me up. I considered dressing up, wanting to be Oliver's dream come true, but I would be pretending. If he doesn't want me as I am, we'll never work anyway. Besides, I don't remember a time when Oliver hasn't looked at me with hunger and desire. With this in mind, I put on a cheery, yellow, eyelet sundress, with spaghetti straps and a flared skirt. Even with this outfit, I still have my hair in a ponytail and I'm wearing flip-flops. It's comfortable and I need the little dash of comfort with the way my stomach is fluttering.

The car rolls to a stop in front of Oliver's gorgeous house. I'm always in awe of it, ever since the moment he first brought me here, it felt like home. The door opens and I see Oliver.

Warning: Core overheating. Nuclear meltdown imminent.

My man is seriously fucking hot. H.O.T—*HOT!* He's wearing a black t-shirt that stretches over his muscled chest and biceps, boot cut jeans, and flip-flops, like me. I lick my lips at the delicious sight; I could eat him from head to toe. I take a step forward and am grateful I brought an extra pair of panties because the ones I'm wearing are already soaked.

He meets me halfway down the steps and gathers me up into his arms, lifting me off of my feet, and kisses me senseless. Relief floods through me, knowing he still wants my body, but I can't help wondering if he still wants to marry me. "I'm so happy you're here, baby," he mumbles against my lips. What little was left of me that hadn't already melted is now molten lava.

"Um, me too." I don't know what the hell is wrong with me, but I blush. He pulls back and seems to drink in the sight of me, as though he is desperately thirsty. There is a lightness about him I don't think I've ever seen before. It's sexy as hell.

He sets me down and takes my hand, gently guiding me up the steps. "I have a surprise for you," he announces. I can hear the excitement in his voice and it sets my tummy aflutter again. We enter the house, and he keeps walking until we reach the big, beautiful kitchen. *I can't wait to bake in here.* Um, that's new. I hate to cook. I look around. Okay, I'd cook in this kitchen. Especially if it was *my* kitchen.

There are three wicker baskets on one of the two large islands in the center of the room. Oliver hands me the smallest one, and takes the others, then he smiles brightly and lifts his chin towards the back door, encouraging me to go out. Once we are outside, I stop to lift my face to the afternoon sun and enjoy the soft breeze. Opening my eyes, I scan the property. It really is gorgeous here.

"Get a move on, baby. We don't have all day and I've got a lot of plans for you."

A shiver rolls down my spine and it has nothing to do with the wind. In fact, it's gotten quite warm in the last two minutes. "Lead the way."

He walks us down to the lake I remember seeing when he first gave me a tour of the house and lands. It's surprisingly clear and the neatly trimmed grass is soft, tempting me to remove my sandals and wiggle my toes in it.

So, I do. Oliver laughs when he notices what I'm doing and winks at me.

Oliver sets the baskets down and lifts one, pulling out a thick quilt and spreading it over the ground. A gigantic smile bursts onto my face. "A picnic?"

He glances at me and nods, seeming extremely satisfied with my expression. "I thought this was better than a stuffy, formal meal. Now get your sweet, little ass over here and help me get the food out. I'm starving."

I practically skip the rest of the way to the blanket and plop down, opening my basket to see what's inside. By the time it's all laid out, I realize it's a feast of my favorite foods. So far, I rate this as the best date ever. Oliver's cache of brownie points is overflowing.

We spend the next couple of hours sitting side by side and munching on the fabulous spread of dishes and treats. We talk about all of the things we love and he asks how my current project is going. I wrinkle my nose. "I'm having a rough time with this one. I'm eons past my deadline and the story simply won't quit. Every time I think it's done, there is a little bit more."

From there, he begins to quiz and question all about my process, the business, etc. Not once do I detect a smidgen of boredom or a lack of interest in what I'm talking about. I know I'm about to regret my decision, but it's only fair, so I ask about his work, as well.

This is when I eat crow. More so than I've already eaten, considering my eleven engaged or married sisters. He's telling me about various projects and I had no idea his business encompassed such a vast array of departments. Some of the goals they are working towards could change the world and not only am I fascinated, but I'm also so proud of Oliver. I hope our kids have his smarts. And looks. And, well, everything that is Oliver.

He checks his watch and looks at me. "Are you ready to pack it in? I have some other things planned, but if you want to stay, we'll do whatever makes you happy."

If words could get you pregnant, I'd probably be having triplets. Oliver Hudson is a walking advertisement for sex. Scratch that. Oliver is walking sex, period. And, I can't wait for the lifetime of experiences that await me by spending forever with him. "You went through all this trouble; I'd like to do whatever it is you have in mind."

Oliver grips me around the waist and lifts, I land square in his lap, facing him, with my legs spread on either side of his. He rubs his nose with mine in an Eskimo kiss and I can't stop the sigh that falls from my lips. "Baby, nothing I do for you is trouble," he rumbles, his voice low and serious. "Haven't you figured it out yet, Pippa? I love you and I'll do whatever it takes to have you. Anything and everything it requires, I'll do happily if, at the end of the day, I have you."

My nose stings and my throat gets scratchy as I fight the tears welling up inside me. I don't deserve him, but I'm keeping him.

Celibacy is a four letter word.

I take a deep breath and open the door to the office I created for Pippa. Theoretically, I know she'll love it, but the nerves creep in anyway. I mentally pat myself on the back for the picnic, though. She'd loved it, and after I made it very clear that she is the most important person in my life, we made out like teenagers for about a half hour. She didn't admit she loved me—yet. But, I am determined to hear it before the night is over.

We'd packed up and brought everything back to the house and I'd tied a blindfold over her face, telling her I had another surprise. She giggled adorably the whole time I was leading her to this room. "Okay, baby. You can take off the blindfold," I whisper from right behind her, my hands on her hips, holding her close. She whips the silk sash over her head and gasps. I set my chin on her shoulder and grin. "What do you think?"

"Is—is this for me?" she asks hesitantly.

"Of course it's for you, baby. I don't think this office would help my image with my clients." My voice becomes husky and dark as I say, "Of course, I do intend to make very good use of that desk. I made sure it was nice and sturdy when I bought it."

Pippa spins, breaking my hold and throwing her arms around my neck. "I love it!" Her mouth lands firmly on mine and I bask in her happiness. Her tongue traces the seam of my lips tentatively and I open my mouth with a groan, but don't take control of the kiss, content to let her explore. She's never kissed anyone but me (a good thing because I didn't care for the idea of another person alive and knowing what it's like to touch my Pippa) and I want her to know she can do what she wants with me, that her boldness pleases me.

Before long, I have to remind myself of the vow to wait until our wedding night. I need to get the hell away from this desk. Breaking apart from her, we both stand here, staring at each other, our hearts racing and it takes a monumental effort for me to look away.

"What—um—what do you want to do now?" she asks, still catching her breath.

Don't go there, Oliver. Just don't even go there.

I clear my throat, attempting to clear my head of all my dirty thoughts in the process. My throat is now empty. One out of two isn't bad, I guess.

"I thought maybe we'd cuddle up in the theater room and watch a movie." I mentally smack myself on the forehead. *This is just what you need, dickhead (and I do mean that literally), your girl pressed up against you, on a couch, in the dark. Real smart move there, stiff dick.* I'm not sure I can handle it.

But, when Pippa's face lights up, I change my tune, because anything that put's that look on her face is something I'm willing to do. I sweep her up into my arms and walk towards the back of the house where I'd turned an old parlor into a state of the art theater room. She laughs and shakes her head at me, but doesn't try to get down. "I'll even let you pick the movie," I say with a quick kiss to her sweet lips.

Getting through the movie is a test of my will-power, and I think I've earned seven A plusses for this. As the credits roll on the action flick she picked out (Yes, I'm marrying the perfecting fucking woman), she yawns and stretches, her gorgeous breasts thrusting out, begging to be sucked on. Okay, time to move on to our regularly scheduled program and then get Pippa the fuck home before I drop my grade down to an F.

"Hey," I say quietly, "you up for one more surprise?"

Pippa laughs, and the sound is like music to me, every note is different, but it's the perfect symphony every time I hear it. "Oliver, if this day is any indication, I don't think I'll ever turn down your surprises."

I grin and wink at her. "I'll remember you said that."

We walk hand in hand to the second floor of the house, where there is a large outdoor veranda. It's a rectangular area that sits directly over the kitchen, with white rod iron rails around the edge, and it has several different arrangements of comfortable outdoor furniture. After settling Pippa on a love seat, I go about lighting a fire in the little pit in front of her.

She's always had a sweet tooth and when I roll out a cart with all of the fixings for S'mores, I know I've scored another perfect grade. "Oliver, this is amazing." She looks at me oddly. "Why haven't we ever done any of this before?"

I shrug, feeling sheepish and trying to play it off with nonchalance. "I wanted to do these things in our home, with my fiancée or wife. You weren't ready." Sitting down next to her, I put a marshmallow on a long, metal roaster and hand it to her.

The corners of her mouth turn down. "But, I'm not either of those things."

I sigh and give her a reproving look. "Do I need to remind you of the facts, baby?" I ask, raising an eyebrow. She looks a little confused and I enlighten her by repeating my words from the day we made the deal. "You're going to be my wife and then I'm going to fuck my kid into you the minute we say I do. It simply is, Pippa. So stop fighting it."

"Who said I'm fighting it anymore?" she asks quietly. The implications of her question hang thick and heavy in the air.

"Pippa?" I question, not sure what to think.

"Maybe if you asked me, instead of ordering me to marry you, you'd know how I feel about it."

"But, you might say no," I argue. I didn't go through all of this so she could have the opportunity to decline. There is no way I am going to wake up the morning after tomorrow without my thoroughly fucked wife in bed with me. I wanted to spend tonight wooing her, but it was always going to have the same result. If only that jackass, Wilhelm, had stuck around to help.

"It's a risk you take when you propose." She looks away and sees her marshmallow has lit on fire. She blows it out and as I sit here contemplating her words; she starts to put her treat together.

"Do you love me, Pippa?" I finally ask. The question seems to take her off guard, and she stares at me with an open mouth and frightened eyes. "Why does loving me scare you, baby?"

"Loving you isn't what scares me, Oliver. It's saying it out loud, giving you the knowledge that you have this much power over me. I want the choice to bind myself to you, not be shackled."

My mind is so thoroughly in the gutter from wanting her all night and denying myself, that I almost miss the point of her comment, being stuck on the idea of silk binding and fur-lined shackles. *Down boy.* I promised I would do anything for her.

I ask her one more time, hoping we can reach a compromise. "Do you love me, Pippa? If you do, then I need you to trust me, to have faith in how I feel for you. That I love who you are and would never try to change you."

She sniffles a little and a few tears slide down her cheeks. "Yes," she says it so low that I almost miss it. I stay still and silent, hoping it will prompt her to say it again. "Yes, I love you, Oliver."

Nothing in the world will ever be as sweet as those words coming from Pippa St. Claire. Actually, there is one. This can only be topped by Pippa Hudson.

How do the mighty fall? Love knocks them on their ass.

━━━∞━━━

PIPPA

I said it. I've given myself to Oliver completely. I don't feel panic. There is no fear. I only feel free, as though a great burden has been lifted off of my heart. And, the look on Oliver's face will be burned into my memory forever. He looks as though he just stepped through the gates of heaven. I expect him to haul me into his arms and kiss the daylights out of me; I am greatly anticipating it. But, he picks up my hand and turns it over, kissing the palm, and replacing it in my lap. My brain starts sputtering, though it hasn't reached my mouth yet. Doesn't "I love you" usually give a closing act involving a grand kiss and a finale?

"Have patience, baby." He grins, obviously seeing my perplexed state. "I'll be right back." He walks away. And still, I sit here in a speechless state of shock, which is quickly turning into disgruntlement.

He returns a minute later with a small, black velvet bag and puts it into the previously kissed palm, before sitting close to me again. There is an air of anticipation about him; I can almost see it pulsing around him. I pull the ribbon tying it together and open the little pouch. Turning it over, something hard and cool falls into my waiting hand.

It's a little book, made of varying colors of quartz and it hangs from a beautiful chain. Oliver reaches out and turns it over, before pushing my hand close to my face, encouraging me to inspect it closer. I then notice each side of the little "book" is inscribed. One side says, *The greatest love story of all*, and the other says, *Was the day I fell in love with you*.

"Oliver it's—I don't know what to say. It's beautiful." I'm crying now and I don't even bother to try and stop.

"Open it." The minute he says it, I spy the tiny hinges and catch. It's a locket.

Flipping the lock up, I open the book into two halves. A ring rests in each side. One is a thick, platinum band with diamond chips every few centimeters, all around it. It's clearly a masculine ring and I know in an instant how perfect it is for Oliver. The other ring makes me breathless, which then morphs into choking due to all of my tears. I wave Oliver off when he starts to look worried. "I'm fine. I swear, I'm ok," I say with a watery smile. "I'm the best ever."

The band of the ring is pavé diamonds all the way around, and another circle of them around the round diamond in the middle. From all the years of listening to my sister talk about jewelry, I'm pretty confident I'm staring at three karats-ish. It's completely stunning, but even more, it's exactly what I would have picked for myself.

I hear the sound of Oliver taking a deep breath, and I look up to see him holding out his hand, palm up. I'm tempted to hold the ring close and not let him take it, but then images of me as Gollum, petting the ring and talking to it, prompt me to hand it over with a sigh.

Oliver closes his hand around it and stands up, then he faces me and goes down to one knee. "Philippa St. Claire, I could make all the flowery speeches in the world, but they would all boil down to one thing; you're mine. So, I'm going to skip them." He pauses and his eyes narrow in warning. "Will you marry me?"

I consider teasing him, but decide it would be a really bitchy thing to do. Instead, I tackle him while screaming yes, then kiss the daylights out of him. See what I mean? Grand kiss and a heart-pumping finale playing so loud it threatens to burst your ear drums. But, you don't care because you're too busy being enthralled by the epic kiss.

We break for air and he starts to slide the ring on then halts. "What about everything else?"

"Everything else?" What is he talking about?

"You're going to have my babies," he states.

"I can live with that," I say in a serious tone, though I'm sure he can see the humor in my eyes because he smirks and starts to slide it on—oh, for the love of... "What now?"

He gives me a speculative glance, once again holding the ring away. "You know this means you have to honor and obey? Emphasis on the obey, Pippa."

"Now you're just pushing it, Oliver."

His grin rivals the sun and when the ring is finally resting all the way on my finger, it's the most comforting and addictive shackle in the world.

Dearly beloved, I need to fuck my wife, so hurry this shit up

~~~

Oliver

I'm pretty sure I just ended up on my mother-in-law's hit list.

After Pippa agreed to marry me, the plan was to take her home and then pick her up to get married today. At the last minute, I realized what a chance I was taking by sending her home. Not a chance on Pippa, no, I was worried Marianne St. Claire, her mother, would find out about my plan and keep Pippa hostage until she'd been allowed to put together a wedding.

Not. Happening.

I put a mental chastity belt on her and put her in a guest room.

Far. Far. Away.

I considered putting her in our room, and I would sleep elsewhere, but I knew, just the thought of her in our bed . . . I'd be fucked. No, let me rephrase. *She'd* be fucked. I spent the night tossing and turning, cursing out Wilhelm because I should have been in a fantasy with Pippa, naked.

After all the help I gave her sisters, I never expected to be sold out. It doesn't matter if they don't know I was behind it, could I get some loyalty here? But, here I am, facing a mother on a mission, determined to keep me from marrying my woman until she gets her way, while her sisters look on with a mixture of guilt and laughter. Their men, however, are full of understanding and sympathy. And, yet, not one of those cowards step forward to help me out. Let's not forget Pippa, who is standing behind me, laughing her pretty little, soon to be red, ass off.

Finally, to avoid manhandling Marianne, I turn to Preston and give one last attempt at diplomacy. I glare at him. "I've proven my worth, and I'm not waiting any longer." I narrow my eyes in warning.

Preston flattens his lips, his eyes sparkling, clearly trying to keep from smiling as he turns to his wife. "Sweetheart, I think it's safe to say Oliver will be marrying Philippa today. If you want to attend the wedding, I suggest you step aside and simply let it happen. If you push it, or threaten him with a dungeon again, my guess is he'll be out the door on the way to the nearest country with no extradition agreement."

"Mom." Pippa's amused voice chimes in from behind me. "Dad's right. Besides, I want to get married today." Looks like Pippa just redeemed herself enough to get out of her spanking. "But, Oliver and I would be more than happy to let you throw us a reception." *I take it back.* I give Pippa a dirty look, shaking my head vigorously. She ignores me and, damn it, I suddenly don't give a fuck what I have to suffer through if I can just fucking marry my woman in the next fifteen minutes!

Marianne looks like she is considering her options and I decide to stop that shit right now. "Attending the wedding and a reception. Final offer. Take it or leave it," I growl. Yeah, I don't wait for her decision. I pick up Pippa and walk around Marianne while she sputters.

Now, let me be clear, my relationship with Pippa, my

desire to marry her, it isn't all a ploy to get her in bed. Although, I know it may seem like it right now. However, I'd like to point out how long I've waited and remind you how romantic I've been. So, give me and my shriveled up blue balls a little understanding. Why am I telling you this? So you don't judge me for almost punching the priest when he chooses to use the longer of the two marriage ceremonies. Also, for the fact that after I kissed the fuck out of my bride, I didn't give her a minute with her family. I simply threw her over my shoulder and stalked out the nearest exit, with Pippa giggling the whole way.

Out of all of the things I considered for our wedding night, I found the most appealing to be returning to our home, making love for the first time in our bed, sharing our first night of our life together in the place where we would live it. We get in a car at the church and I tell the driver to take us home. Pippa sighs and when I look at her, her face is soft and dreamy, and I know I made the right call.

At the house, I instruct the driver to let us out in the front, circle drive. We exit the back and I sweep my wife up into my arms to the sweet sound of her laughter. I carry her into the entryway of the house and set her down. She looks all around, taking it in, and prompting me to ask, "Does it look different?"

She smiles and cocks her head to the side. "A little. I suppose anything does when it becomes yours. I'm looking at this room now, thinking about when our children will run through this door after school, the holidays when our families will enter here, the day our daughter's first date arrives—"

"—No way," I bark. "No dating. I'll agree to have girls, but only if there is a no dating rule. Otherwise, boy. All boys."

Pippa rolls her eyes and throws her hands in the air, exasperation written all over her face. "Such an ego. You can't pick the gender of our babies, Oliver. And, I'm not going to let you keep our daughter or daughters sequestered away in some tower like the villain in a fairy tale."

"We'll just see about that," I mutter under my breath, then louder, I say, "It's time to get started on those boys you're going to have, baby." I grin at her annoyed expression and pull her to me, kissing her like it's our first. In a way, it is. The first kiss at the wedding doesn't really count. This kiss, the first in our home, as husband and wife, it's the start of an amazing journey. It's also the straw that breaks the camel's back and in no time, I've got Pippa cradled against my chest as I jog up the steps and down the hall to the master suite. Stepping inside, I inhale deeply and release it slowly, endeavoring to calm myself. This is going to be slow and special, even if it kills me. *It just might.*

I take Pippa straight to the turned down bed and lay her down in the center, remove her soft yellow heels, then stand back and admire the view. Damn. She is so fucking beautiful. And, all mine. "This is the beginning of one of my favorite fantasies," I tell her. "My wife, the love of my life, in our bed, waiting for me." She raises her arms to me and my heart skips a beat. I kick off my own shoes and lay down on the bed next to her, me on my side, and Pippa on her back. She drops her arms, looking at me in confusion. "I've waited my whole life for you, Pippa. I'm not going to be rushed. I'm going to savor every moment with you, starting with our wedding night."

Pippa's olive complexion flushes with a tinge of pink, her face bright with happiness. I run a single finger from her collar bone, down the center of her body, until I reach the apex of her thighs. She'd chosen to wear a cream colored, summery dress, with knee-length, flowy skirt and I appreciate the choice when I hook a finger under the hem and drag her skirt up to her waist.

I stop breathing. *Holy fucking hell.* Pippa has on white, nearly see-through, underwear with tiny bows on the sides and one in the center. My beautiful wife is wrapped up like a delectable present, just waiting for me to open and taste my mouth-watering treat. I bunch her skirt and take one of her hands, placing it over the material so she knows to hold it up. Slipping a finger into her panties, I dip it into her pussy and fuck, she's soaked. I draw the digit out, torturously slow, straight up the middle, between her lips, right over her little bud. She shudders and moans, watching me as I lick her essence from my finger.

She tastes like sweet spices and something more, something that is simply Pippa. "Damn, you taste fucking delicious, baby." Leaning up, I work her panties down her legs, leaving her bare and glistening with her arousal. I move to kneel between her legs, pushing them wide and take the time to admire her pussy, so pink and wet. I lick my lips in anticipation and glance up at my wife. She's blushing fire-engine red, seemingly nervous and a little uncomfortable.

I crawl up her body and kiss her, surrounding her in a haze of lust and desire as it explodes from the chemistry sparking at the touch of our lips. She sighs and melts into it and when I end the kiss, she's flushed for an entirely different reason. "Baby, who does this gorgeous body belong to?" I ask sternly. She looks like she might argue, so I prove my point by sliding a finger inside her, pump it in and out a couple of times, then drag it up to circle her clit, making her moan. "Who owns this body, Pippa?"

"Ah, ah, you!" she cries out, her hips chasing after my hand, trying to force contact where she really wants it. But, I studiously keep from touching her little bundle of nerves, not ready for her to come.

"Very good, baby," I purr. "I don't want you to be self-conscious, but most importantly"—I grip her chin, making sure she hears me—"you have nothing to be embarrassed about when it comes to what we do together in the bedroom." I smirk. "Or anywhere else I choose to make you moan.

"And," I continue. "Right now, I need to taste your sweet pussy. You're going to be a good girl and hold your legs open for me." I sit back and bend her knees, pushing them to her chest, widen them as far as possible and guide her hands to grip under her thighs. "Don't let go," I instruct, my face conveying that I'm not messing around and expect her to obey.

Sliding my hands under her ass, I lift her pussy up and lean forward to slowly lick from bottom to top, circle her clit, and back down.

"Oh! Ah!" Pippa cries out, partly in shock, but mostly her voice is thick with pleasure.

"*Mmm*, it's sexy as fuck when you're loud, baby. I want to know what you like, what drives you crazy, what makes you scream my name." I repeat the lick, this time, plunging my tongue into her hole on the way back down.

"Oliver! Oh!"

"Interesting," I mumble cheekily. I do it all again, faster, several times.

"Oh! Yes! Ah! Ah!"

Fuck it. I'm not waiting. I replace my tongue with my finger, curling it into just the right spot, and suck hard on her clit. She screams at the top of her lungs, and I hungrily eat at her, prolonging her orgasm as long as possible, lapping up the juices gushing from her pussy. I'm a greedy fucker, so when she starts to float back down, I redouble my efforts, wringing a second orgasm from her, keeping my eyes trained on her. When she screams my name, I almost fucking come in my pants. Finally letting up, I sit back up and wipe her essence from my chin, licking my fingers clean. "I think I've got a new favorite snack."

"Umm-hmm..." Pippa hums, evidently, having lost the

ability to form words. I'd pat myself on the back if I wasn't too busy beginning to undress her, eager to feel her naked body underneath mine. She's languid and sated, but manages to lift her hips so I can get her dress off. Lastly, I sit her up and reach around her back to undo the catch on her white, strapless bra. I pull it out from between us before tossing it over my shoulder and lowering her back down to the bed.

Magnificent. There really is no other word to describe Pippa's breasts. James once told me "There's a shortage of perfect breasts in this world." I have to agree with him, but Pippa is definitely at the top of the list. They are round and full, just the right size to fill my palms. Her long, dark hair fell forward while she was sitting up and it streams down her torso, playing peekaboo with her firm nipples.

I quickly undress, dropping my clothes off the side of the bed, then shift until I'm on my knees, straddling Pippa's legs. Her eyes are glued to my cock, as it bounces against my stomach with my movements. It's long and thick, and I can tell she's worried about the fit from the fear in her eyes.

I cup her face and look deeply into her rich, sable eyes. "Do you trust me?" She nods without thought and love for her fills me, shocking because I didn't think there was any room left. "I'll take care of you. Trust me to make this special and as painless as possible, okay?" The fear begins to recede, and she smiles shyly, nodding again.

Tenderly, I push her hair away, baring her chest completely, then find I was right, when I cup her breasts, they just barely spill out of my hands. I massage them gently and her hard nipples scrape my palms, the sensation causing her to moan. The picture she paints has come leaking from the tip of my cock and I know I've got to have her soon, or I'll be wasting it when it should be inside her, making our baby.

I squeeze her breasts a little rougher now, watching her carefully to make sure it pleases her. She squirms and her lower body brushes against my balls. I'm minutes away from coming all over her stomach. But, I want to make sure she is truly ready for me, so this is as painless as possible. I pinch her nipples between my thumb and forefinger, then twist and pluck them. Damn, she is so fucking responsive.

I change my position, coming down over her body, lying in the middle of her legs, and when my cock rests firmly nestled against her bare pussy, I groan in absolute rapture, it feels better than any fantasy. My mouth seeks out a rosy tip and I suckle her nipple, alternating with long, deep pulls, then switch to her other breast. Pippa is becoming more and more anxious and her writhing is actually hardening my cock even further. I have no fucking clue how it's possible, it seemed like my skin was already stretched as far as possible. Yet, I feel it tighten even more and I wince at the pain.

I can't take another second of not being inside her. Bracing myself on my elbows, I pick my hips up to perfectly line up my cock with her pussy. The tip is bathed in her heat and it feels fucking amazing. With one arm, I guide one of her legs around my waist and then do the same with the other. Her eyes are wide and a little frightened, clearing away the mists of desire that were just there. "Trust me, baby. I love you," I whisper as I start to push inside her.

It's a tight fit. She's so damn small, and I remind myself over and over to go slow. "Fuck, Pippa. You're so damn tight. Like a vice squeezing my cock, it's so fucking good." Little by little, I work my way in, until I feel the evidence of her virginity. I'm not going to lie, I'm mentally banging on my chest and shouting like a lunatic that this woman is mine and mine alone.

"Hey," I say softly and wait until she meets my gaze. "I love you."

She practically melts right before my eyes, all of her muscles relaxing. It's exactly what I was hoping would happen. I kiss her and plunge in hard enough to break the thin barrier. She tenses, but I keep kissing her and she soon relaxes again, her body welcoming mine. At this point, I'm far enough in that her walls are clamping down on me, sucking me into her instead of trying to force me out. Once I'm all the way in, seated to the hilt inside her, I pause to let her adjust. Her muscles spasm and my eyes practically roll back into my head at the exquisite pleasure rocketing through me.

I start to move slowly, gradually picking up strength in my thrusts, watching her for any indication I might be hurting her, but her face is awash with bliss, her hands gripping my biceps with surprising strength. With long, even strokes I guide us up, up, refusing when my body or Pippa's urge me to speed up. This isn't about fucking; this is about love. It's about making love to my wife, savoring the moment when we become one for the first time. At last, we reach the tip of the mountain and I glide through her slick pussy until I'm buried so fucking deep, I can feel her cervix.

"It's time for you to come, Pippa. Open up for me, baby, I'm going to fill you with my come until I know you've got our child growing inside you." She whimpers as her body thrashes with unspent energy. Taking one of her nipples into my mouth, I suck it hard, while I use two fingers to pinch her clit. Pippa's back arches, coming up off the bed, her hands clawing at my back as she screams, exploding with a shuddering orgasm.

I pump my hips three more times before planting myself fully inside and knowing her womb is in the prime place to accept the hot jets of my seed erupting from my cock, I shout as my orgasm rips through my body. The spurts come to an end and I collapse on top of her, careful not to crush her under my weight. We're both panting, gasping for air as our hearts race.

But, I'm not done yet, and my still rock hard cock clearly

agrees. "Now that I've made love to you, I'm going to fuck you," I growl into Pippa's ear. She sucks in a ragged breath and her pussy clenches around my cock. She seems to like the idea. I clasp her wrists and guide her arms up on either side of her head, and wrap her fingers around the headboard. "Hold tight, baby. If you let go, you're going to get your ass spanked. Understood?" Her eyes widen, a mixture of curiosity and heat. I raise an eyebrow and wait.

"Yes," she croaks.

"Yes, what?" I want to make sure we are very clearly on the same page.

She clears her throat and answers, "Yes, I understand. I won't let go."

"Good girl," I coo before taking her mouth in a tongue-tangling kiss. I think I'd still be lost in this kiss if my cock weren't pulsing with need again. "Uhhh," I groan. "Your pussy is so tight, I can feel my cock stretching it with every heartbeat."

She moans and I'm starting to realize my Pippa has a taste for my dirty mouth. "Do you want my cock, baby? Do you want me to fuck you hard until you are screaming so loud the neighbors know you're in the throes of orgasm?"

Pippa sucks in a breath and her body arches into mine, her breasts pressing against my chest so I can feel her nipples, hardened with lust. Taking advantage of her position, I bite one, then soothe it with a lick, before sucking on it in rhythm with my thrusts as I begin to move again.

"Ah! Oh, Oliver! I—ah!"

The sound of my name sparks something inside me and the beast inside me claws to the surface. Grabbing her legs, I throw them over my shoulders, and pick her ass up, then slam into her so hard the headboard bangs against the wall.

"Yesss! Oliver! Oh, yes!" she hollers as she comes violently.

I'm all animal now, nothing civilized remains as I pound

my cock into her snug pussy. My grip on her ass is going to leave bruises and I'm perversely turned on by the thought, knowing I've marked her. The bed crashes against the wall, her screams are ringing in the air—all of it simply burns the fire raging inside me. I throw my head back, my voice hoarse as I yell, wild, almost unhinged, "Shit—Pippa—oh fuck—Oh fuck, Pippa! Oh! Oh, fuck! Oh FUCK!"

I'm craving her orgasms like an addiction and I can't help working her up to another one. The sound of her coming is the strongest aphrodisiac in the world. I'll never get enough.

Suddenly, I feel her clutch my ass, pulling me in deeper and I automatically raise my hand and bring it down on her ass. "Hands!" I shout. I lift my head and look into her eyes as she grabs the headboard again. Her eyes are frantic, her hips bucking, meeting my every powerful drive into her.

"Again."

She says it so timidly, I almost miss it. "You want me to spank your ass again, Pippa?" I growl. She moans and nods her head. I slap her opposite cheek, leaving a pink handprint behind and it's hot as fuck. Her knuckles are white as she holds on, her arms tensed, and her pussy is clenched so hard, if it weren't for how fucking drenched she is, I don't think I'd be able to pull out. "Baby, you're so ready, aren't you?" I pant. "You want me to bury myself deep, deep inside you until you're coming around my cock?"

"Yes! Oliver, oh yes! Oh fucking hell, yes! YES!"

That does it. I pull out and take her hands from the headboard, flip her around to her hands and knees, before returning them to their spot. I ram back into her with every last bit of my strength, over and over, and though I know she probably won't be able to walk tomorrow, I can't stop.

I put my hands around her and palm her breasts, jerking her upright, and pinch her nipples, twisting them hard. Then I let go of one to slap her pussy, setting her off, and it's like my body takes it as permission. After I drop her back down to her hands, grab her hips, and slam into her two more times, I spiral up and hit the fucking roof as I orgasm so hard, I'm dizzy with it. "Fuck yes, baby! Squeeze that pussy. Yes—oh fuck, Pippa—fuck, fuck! Yeah, baby, even mo—fuck!" I feel like I'm going to break into pieces, my heart will stop, and I'll simply drop dead from pleasure.

Walking is overrated.

PIPPA

I don't know what that was. Earth shattering. Mind blowing. Those don't even come close to describing what just happened to me. I'm lying prone on the bed, with Oliver collapsed on top of me. I can feel his heartbeat going a mile a minute and he's sucking in large amounts of air, his body still shuddering with aftershocks.

He finally seems to realize he might be crushing me and rolls to the side, dragging me with him, so we are spooning, with him still inside me. "Is it supposed to be like that?" I ask quietly. He's always taken me to new heights with his fingers, and then with his mouth today, it was fucking amazing. But, when he's inside me? This was unreal. I can barely move a muscle, like they are made of pudding.

"It won't always be quite like that, so frantic and crazy," he answers as he nuzzles his nose in my hair. "Sometimes, we'll make love, sometimes we'll fool around, sometimes we'll fuck, and whatever else we discover. But, it will always be love, which means, it will always be amazing."

I sigh, so happy and content, and exhausted as all hell. I can barely keep my eyes open.

"I was really rough," he says, and I can hear the concern in his tone. "You're going to be very sore tomorrow."

"Eh," I shrug. "Walking is overrated."

His chest rumbles before a chuckle leaves his lips.

"Oliver?"

"Hmmm?"

"I know this sounds crazy but, did you have something to do with my sisters all finding love over the last two weeks?"

He's silent for a long time, and I think maybe he isn't going to answer. "It wasn't me, so much as Wilhelm." I start to ask what he means but he reaches down and pulls the covers over us. "Another time. Go to sleep, baby," he whispers, kissing my temple and I yawn, but try to disguise it. "There is no reason to stay awake; we have our whole lives together."

"I'm afraid if I fall asleep, I'll wake up and this will all have been a fantasy," I admit.

Oliver doesn't laugh like I expected him to and it warms me all over. Instead, he kisses my head again and snuggles me closer. "Trust me, this isn't a fantasy, Pippa. This is our reality."

PIPPA

Five years later...

It's a beautiful night to sit outside and it's a rare night to have all three of our kids in bed and asleep. Oliver and I are sitting out in our favorite spot on the veranda, making S'mores.

"Okay," I say sternly. "You've put me off for five freaking years. I'm not going to let you seduce me into waiting any longer." He grins salaciously knowing he could if he really wanted to, because I am weak. I glare at him until he drops the smile.

He sighs. "It's going to sound crazy and if you did believe me, I was afraid you would think what we have isn't real."

I scoff, but he looks so serious, it sobers me. "Oliver, I think it's safe to say, after five years and three"—I look down at my four-month baby bump—"and a half kids, I'm pretty confident about how much you love me. And, the dirty diapers keep me firmly grounded in reality."

He chuckles, seeming a little lighter. "Well, after your little stunt with the law, I found this key..."

When Oliver finishes the story, I'm pretty speechless. He

watches me silently, likely wondering if I believe him. "Wow. What a little shit that key ended up being."

Oliver stares at me for a minute, stunned. Then he bursts into laughter and pulls me over onto his lap. "I love you."

I smile and kiss him tenderly. "I love you, too."

He cocks his head like he always does when he has an idea. "I wonder if this story would make a good novel for you?"

I think about it for a few minutes, then shake my head. "One book that is nothing but twelve happily ever afters? Who would buy it?"

Also by Elle Christensen

Silver Lake Shifters

An Unexpected Claim: Nathan & Peyton (Book 1) – Available Now!

An Uncertain Claim: Nathan & Peyton (Book 2) – Available Now!

An Unending Claim: Nathan & Peyton (Book 3) - Available Now!

A Promised Claim: Asher & Savannah (Book 4) - TBD

A Forbidden Claim (Book 4) – TBD

A Vengeful Claim (Book 5) – TBD

The Fae Guard Series

Protecting Shaylee (Book 1) – Available Now!

Loving Ean (Book 2) – Available Now!

Chasing Hayleigh (Book 3) – Available Now!

A Very Faerie Christmas (Book 4) – Available Now!

Saving Kendrix (Book 5) – Available Now!

Forever Fate: (Book 6) – Available Now!

The Fae Legacy (A Fae Guard Spin-off)

Finding Ayva (Book 1) – Coming 2022

The Slayer Witch Trilogy

The Slayer Witch (Book 1) - Summer 2022

The Wolf, the Witch, and the Amulet (Book 2) – Summer 2022

Stone Butterfly Rockstars

Another Postcard (Book 1) – Available Now!

Rewrite the Stars (Book 2) – Coming 2022

Daylight (Book 3) – TBD

Just Give Me a Reason (book 4) – TBD

All of Me (Book 5) – TBD

Miami Flings

Spring Fling – Available Now!

All I Want (Miami Flings & Yeah, Baby Crossover) – Available Now!

Untitled – TBD

Ranchers Only Series

Ranchers Only – Available Now!

The Ranchers Rose – Available Now!

Ride a Rancher – Available Now!

When You Love a Rancher – Available Now!

Untitled – TBD

Happily Ever Alpha

Until Rayne – Available Now!

Until the Lighting Strikes – Available Now!

Until the Thunder Rolls – Coming 2022

Standalone Books

Love in Fantasy – Available Now!

Say Yes (A military Romance) – Available Now!

Bunny Vibes – Available Now!

Fairytale Wishes (Mermaid Kisses Collaboration) - Available Now!

Books Co-authored with Lexi C. Foss

Crossed Fates (Kingdom of Wolves) – Available Now!

First Kiss of Revenge (Vampire Dynasty Trilogy Book 1) - 2022

First Bite of Pleasure (Vampire Dynasty Trilogy Book 2) – TBD

First Taste of Blood (Vampire Dynasty Trilogy Book 3) – TBD

Books Co-authored with K. Webster

Erased Webster (Standalone Novel) – Available Now!

Give Me Yesterday (Standalone Novel) – Available Now!

If you enjoy quick and dirty and SAFE, check out Elle Christensen and Rochelle Paige's co-written books under the pen name Fiona Davenport!

Website

About the Author

About Elle Christensen

I'm a lover of all things books and have always had a passion for writing. Since I am a sappy romantic, I fell easily into writing romance. I love a good HEA! I'm a huge baseball fan, a blogger, and obsessive reader.

My husband is my biggest supporter and he's incredibly patient and understanding about the people is my head who are fighting with him for my attention.

I hope you enjoy reading my books as much as I enjoyed writing them!

Join Elle Christensen's newsletter to receive a couple of updates a month on new releases and exclusive content. To join, all you need to do is click here.

Website
Newsletter Book+Main

Acknowledgments

So many people to thank, but since I'm so far behind on my deadline, I'll keep this short so I can hit publish!

Ro, I really don't need to say it, do I? Everyone who reads this should thank her for making this book possible.

To my editors, Vanessa and Jacquelyn, thank you for fixing me! It's like my fingers forget how to speak correctly...

Oh, Stacey...it's just so beautiful!!! Champagne Formats brings the insides of my books to life!

Many thanks to Jennifer Munswami for the beautiful cover!

And to Scarlet Dawn for putting this series together and including me as a part of it!

To the many bloggers and readers who support and love me, you are the reason I continue to write! Thank you for reading my stuff!

Printed in Great Britain
by Amazon